A Degree of Wickedness

A Thrilling Tale Collection
By Kimberly Bennett

A Degree of Wickedness

First Edition: September 2011
Printed in the United States of America
ISBN-13: 978-0615511931
ISBN-10: 0615511937

Kimberly Bennett

Acknowledgments

*Thank you to my family, friends
and fans that have stood by my side and encouraged
me with my writing.
I love you all dearly!*

A Degree of Wickedness

A Degree of Wickedness

A Thrilling Tale Collection

By
Kimberly Bennett

A Degree of Wickedness

Kimberly Bennett

Contents

A Degree of Wickedness

Rusalka Lake

The coming night was on the verge of completely blanketing the sky with its darkness. Streaks of pink, gold and flame orange painted the sky with their vibrant colors, signifying that evening was upon us. The air was cooler now and a gentle breeze enveloped my body with its soft caress. I currently sat by Rusalka Lake and waited for the inevitable. I didn't know if the legend was true about this body of water but I hoped and prayed that it was.

Last month I was diagnosed with a form of terminal cancer. I would give you the long and difficult name of the exact illness but at this point it is irrelevant. I literally have an expiration date and the clock is ticking down to my demise rather quickly.

I came to the lake to end my torment; the disease that has ravaged my body, my mind and my soul. I refuse to allow cancer to choose my last day on this earth. I was taking the helm from my disease. Mutiny was on my mind as I had to endure my illness and watch my life disintegrate before me. My family, my hopes, my dreams and my body were all out of my grasp now. The reality was that I was nothing more than a decrepit shell. My illness was eating me alive inside and out. My muscular physique and my natural rugged good looks had diminished drastically; It left me shriveled, weak and on the precipice of death.

Rusalka Lake had been closed to the public for several years now. No one knows the exact circumstances of the closing. Details were sketchy, at best. However, if my memory serves me right I believe the story of events leading to the lake closure involved the mysterious disappearance of three young men from town. All three were approximately twenty years of age; they were good boys. The kind you could take home to Dad and he would have approved. It was said that they came to the lake looking for the Rusalka. I guess the easy way to define a Rusalka would be to say the creature was a siren of the waters; an evil mermaid if you will. Rusalka seduced men to the water's edge with their beauty and then they would grab them and take them to their watery grave. Many don't believe in the mythological creature and many will not know if those young men found what they were looking for. The bodies never turned up and Rusalka Lake was closed forever.

Total darkness engulfed me now. The lake was covered in the evening's inky blackness. The only light I had was a few twinkling stars and a bright, silvery full-moon as I sat by the water's edge on a large boulder. I won't go into details as to how I managed to position myself atop the massive rock. It was quite difficult and if it had not been for the morphine that I had taken just before I drove here, well then I would have never made it to where I was. The cold boulder was an uncomfortable perch but I waited in anticipation for the creature anyways.

Small ripples of water lapped at my feet as they dangled just below the water's surface. I reflected on my life that was cut short, for a moment or two, until the ripples turned into tiny waves. The cool water didn't just massage my feet now but reached upwards towards my calf. The soft churning of the water relaxed me and I waited some more. The wave's height increased and my heart rate did, as well. My thoughts turned to the Rusalka and how I prayed that she was real. I was determined to end my life on my terms and going to a watery grave with the Rusalka as my guide, was what I intended to do. Each wave increased my anxiety and questions flooded what was left of my mind. Could this be her? Would she grasp me in one quick movement and drag me down into a dark and cold abyss? Would she really be beautiful? Or would any beauty she had be an illusion to entice me into her arms for her to complete her wicked task? I was scared and excited at the same time.

A Degree of Wickedness

I felt a slight tugging on my toes. It felt as if little minnows were nibbling and nudging my digits with their tiny mouths. I peered into the water to see who my attackers were. Leaning closer to the water's surface, with the aid of the moonlight, I saw feminine arms reaching up towards me. I extended my hand down into the water and grasp a delicate hand and pulled it towards me. To my surprise, a lovely creature emerged from the water. Her skin was ivory and her hair was dark, long and thick. Her locks clung to her shoulders and upper back as she slithered onto the rock beside me. I gazed at her beauty with amazement. Her breasts were plump and pert. Her waist was tiny and her hips were voluptuous. Her fish tail started just below her hips and stretched down the side of the boulder into the water. The smooth scales on her tail glittered in the moonlight and her feathery fins swished back and forth just below the surface of the water. She was breathtaking. She was a dream come true and I gazed at her beautiful form in disbelief.

We sat for several moments next to each other and stared across the lake. She lifted a hand and gently rested it on my upper thigh. The gesture was sensual and I watched as her fingers traced dainty circular patterns on my leg. I was afraid to look her in the face. I was afraid that she was a dream and that as soon as I made full facial contact she would disappear and leave me to die alone a terrible death at the hands of my disease. The Rusalka reached her other hand up and caressed the side of my face. She cupped my chin and gently urged me to look her in the eyes. I dared to raise my head and eyes towards her. When our eyes met she looked deeply into mine, as if she was reading my every thought. Somehow it seemed that she understood why I was there and the expression of concern that was written on her face solidified my conclusion. I truly believed that she was sympathetic to my plight and was willing to grant my last wish.

We broke our mesmerizing eye contact and she released my chin from her grasp while dropping her hand to her lap. Her other hand still swirled and twirled patterns on my leg. I looked down into the water and watched as she swished her fish tail back and forth. The sound her fins made in the water was relaxing, almost hypnotic. My anxiety had subsided and I was reaching a state of calmness. I felt her watching me as I watched her fins dance underwater. I raised my head and peered into her sparkling dark eyes and it was as if I was peering into her soul. Her gaze was magnetic and I felt a connection was made between us. I couldn't put my finger on it but sitting here with her in this place; I felt like there was hope for me, after all. No, not a hope that meant a cure from my disease but a hope that maybe life on the other side would be better for me. I was prepared to make my journey from this life to the next with the Rusalka as my guide.

I snapped back to reality when I felt the Rusalka pat my leg firmly, signaling that it was time. I watched as she gracefully slid off the boulder and into the water. Her body bobbed in the water like a buoy. She reached up and grasped my hands and pulled me into the water in front of her. The water was cool and soothing and it caressed my body like fresh silken sheets. She released her grip on my hands and wrapped her arms tightly about my neck; drawing me against her waiting body. Her bare breasts rubbed hard against my chest and ignited a fire in my loins. I sighed at the feeling. It had been a long time since I felt desire for a woman. My sickness had not only robbed me of my good looks, but it also took my desire for sexual encounters. I sank into her embrace as my blood coursed with sexual energy. The longer I rested in her arms the greater my arousal became. She looked deep into my eyes and I hers. She moved her face closer to mine so that the tips of our noses touched. She smiled an impish smile and at that moment I just wanted to take her; to make love to her and consummate my desire for her. Her sweet smile turned into a lustful kiss as she locked her luscious lips with mine. I closed my eyelids and reveled in her deliciousness. Her lips felt cool and as she slid her tongue in my mouth, I opened my mouth more. Her tongue felt like an ice cube probing mine. My tongue met hers and they danced the dance of lovers. I was fully aroused and anxious at the thought of a sexual encounter with this creature. I paused in my excitement as I felt something smooth and strong slither its way around my body. The feeling was erotic and I released myself from our passionate kiss, as I opened my eyelids. I noticed that her tail had wrapped itself around me several times from my feet up to my hips. It had coiled around me firmly like a python would its prey. I began to panic and tried to push away but she held me tightly within her grasp. I realized, rather quickly, that this was it. My whole purpose for being here and in her arms was to die, so I gave up my struggle and allowed her to drag me below the water's surface.

To my horror as we descended into the water deeper, her face had turned from being beautiful into something more sinister and evil. The Rusalka's ivory skin peeled off her delicate cheek bones and exposed a skeletal face. Her feminine teeth grew into large protruding fangs that gnashed at me as we continued our descent. Fear struck me hard as I asked myself one final question before my very last breath. Was this really what I wanted?

What a Little Girl Can Do

Jolene moaned as she tried to roll over in bed and look at the time on the clock setting on her nightstand. The red led display informed her that it was ten o'clock in the morning and she needed to get her butt moving if she was going to get her work for the day done.

Jolene eyed the bottle of aspirin she had handy, setting on her night stand beside the clock. She reached slowly for the bottle and let out another moan of regret as she grabbed the bottle and fought the child proof cap off. Jolene dumped two pills into the palm of her hand and popped them in her mouth. She replaced the lid and decided to throw the bottle of aspirin across the room. She watched it hit the wall and drop to the wooden floor at the foot of her bed. Jolene worked up some saliva in her mouth and downed the pills and waited for them to take effect. She sunk back down onto her mattress and pondered the inevitable.

Jolene lay in bed and thought deeply about the events that were going to take place this very day. After twenty minutes of contemplating, she could feel the aspirin working its magic and tried to move again. Her body aches had diminished and it was time for her to get going. She rolled over onto her side and sat up gingerly. Her whole body ached in protest but Jolene couldn't procrastinate any longer. Larry would be home soon and the crap was going to hit the fan. After mentally motivating herself into a sitting position and then onto her feet, she managed to drag herself to the bathroom and clean up a bit before moving on to search her closet for the rifle her father had given her at the age of fifteen.

Jolene found the rifle in the back left corner of the closet and as she grabbed the handle and stood up straight she praised the miracle of science for giving the world aspirin. Her body aches were almost a bittersweet memory. Jolene shut her closet door and gently tossed the gun on her bed. She then turned and made her way over to her dresser, that sat below her windowsill, on the right side of her bed. She rummaged through her drawers for her cut off jeans, a purple tank top with spaghetti straps and a pair of socks. After obtaining her prizes, she backed up and sat back down on her bed to get dressed.

A Degree of Wickedness

Jolene made quick work of her wardrobe. Once she was dressed, Jolene reached down to the corner between the bed and dresser and fetched her tennis shoes. She quickly slipped her footwear on and stood to leave her room. Jolene briefly turned towards her bed to retrieve the rifle and made her way to the door. She shut the door with the gun in hand and headed for the kitchen. Making her way down the short hall, she got a glimpse of her reflection in a mirror on the wall; the one her mother had purchased her before she had passed away of cancer the summer before. Saddened by the memory and disheartened at her appearance, Jolene kept walking. The black eye and split lip didn't look any better than it had last night before she had gone to bed. All Jolene could do was shake her head in disgust at the previous night's drama.

Jolene made it to the kitchen and rooted around the drawers for the shells to her rifle. She had searched three junk drawers before finally finding her treasure box. Carefully, Jolene extracted the shell box from the drawer, shut the drawer and went over to the kitchen table. She sat down and began to load her ticket to freedom. After loading the rifle, Jolene placed the weapon down on the table and went to the cupboards above the sink to find some tea bags and sugar.

After Jolene found the tea bags and sugar, she set about the kitchen to make herself a steaming cup of heaven. When she was finished with her task, Jolene pulled out a chair and sat down. She placed her mug gently on the table and scooted her chair under the table and picked up the pack of smokes and the lighter from the tabletop. She then removed a cigarette from the package and used the lighter to light it up. Jolene tossed the lighter and pack of cigarettes back onto the table and leaned back in her chair. She took a long drag and sighed at the soothing comfort of the nicotine and exhaled while contemplating Larry's return from the county lock up. She watched as steam rose from her mug and swirled around her cigarette smoke. It was as if the cigarette smoke and steam were participating in a romantic dance. They swirled and twirled and tickled each other until Jolene lifted her other hand and waved them away. She lifted her mug and drank deeply from the hot liquid and sat her cup down while swallowing. She tipped her head back and allowed the tea to begin its warming of her core. The warmth traveled from her lips, to her throat and down into her stomach. The tea, teamed with her inhalation of cigarette smoke, relieved her tension.

Larry wasn't going to be happy but at least he will have slept off the alcohol and will be fully aware of the scene that will unfold when he walks through the front door. Jolene was going to show him what a little girl can do.

After a couple of years of mental and physical abuse at the hands of her live in boyfriend, Larry, Jolene had finally had enough. Her mother had pleaded with her to dump Larry and move on after the first episode of violence but Jolene was determined to give him a second and then a third and finally a fourth chance to redeem himself. After last night's drama, Jolene was prepared to do the unthinkable. Larry had to die.

Jolene snapped back to reality and the task at hand. She placed her burning cigarette in the ashtray on the kitchen table, then rose from her chair and strolled outside to the shed closest to the house. The smell of swamp was strong. Heat and humidity allowed the odor of rotting vegetation to weigh heavy on the air. Jolene spent her whole life on this property, so the odor didn't faze her like it did the cottage's few visitors. Jolene opened the shed door and rummaged around for three tarps she knew she put in there last spring when she had painted the living room. A smile crept across her lips when she found what she was looking for. With a couple of hard tugs, the tarps tumbled out of the shed and onto the grass. Jolene bent to picked them up and made her way back to the cottage and to the kitchen dragging them behind her in haste.

Jolene opened the kitchen door from outside and struggled to pull the tarps in. After a few moments and a few moans of irritation, Jolene accomplished her goal. She quickly unrolled the sea of heavy fabric and set to work on placing them strategically in the room. She hung one on the wall opposite the table, where the doorway from the hall was situated. She placed one on the floor in front of the doorway, where she predicted Larry would be standing. Next, Jolene hung the third from the ceiling with a hammer and nails she found in the kitchen junk drawer, the previous evening, which she purposely left out on the kitchen counter.

Happy with her accomplishment she sat down in her chair at the kitchen table for a rest. Jolene looked at the ashtray and was annoyed that her cigarette had gone out. She reached for the pack of smokes and lighter again and lit up another. Jolene tossed her cigarette pack and lighter back onto the table and took a drag and slowly exhaled. She enjoyed smoking. Somehow it seemed to calm her down. After allowing the nicotine to hit her brain and revel in its magic, Jolene relaxed. Now, all she had to do was wait; wait for Larry to come home.

Jolene took another long drag from her cigarette and exhaled. She began to recall the domestic violence that had befallen her at the hands of Larry. He had come home drunk from the local watering hole and began to argue with her over some nonsense that she couldn't even begin to remember. She did remember shooting back some expletives at him, which resulted in the black eye and split lip that she received. After she had taken the blows Larry had dished out to her, Jolene then remembered how Larry threw her to the ground and proceeded to force himself on her. She begged and pleaded for him to stop but all he did was keep on hurting her while mocking her words of distress. Jolene had decided to detach herself emotionally after her physical and verbal efforts to free herself of the violence were wasted on his enormous strength and his sarcastic tone. After Larry was done with Jolene, he rolled off of her and passed out. Jolene crawled into the bedroom and used her phone on her dresser to call the police.

When the police arrived, Larry was still passed out on the floor and Jolene was huddled in a corner of her bedroom by her bed. The police arrested Larry and took him to the station. While the police where at Jolene's, they gave her information on domestic violence and a case number for her to use for any contact that she may make with the authorities concerning her assault. Several pictures were taken of her injuries and she was asked if she wanted an ambulance but she denied medical treatment and escorted them to the door, while explaining that she would be fine with Larry being carted off to jail. The police reluctantly left Jolene alone and took Larry away.

Jolene refocused her mind to the present and took another hit from her cigarette. She was ashamed of herself and knew her mother would be too, had she still been alive. Jolene had made up her mind last night, as she lay in bed and cried herself to sleep, that she wasn't going to be anyone's punching bag, ever again. That's when pride and anger took their foothold in Jolene.

Jolene jumped back to reality when she heard Larry's truck making its way down the long and winding driveway to her ancestral cottage. The cottage was small but just big enough for Jolene. There was no more room for Larry. His time to leave had come. Jolene heard the gravel crunch beneath the old truck tires and as it came to a hard stop, she then heard the grind of the gravel and the squeal of protest from the brakes. The truck door squeaked open and next came a loud slam of the rusted out door that made Jolene flinch in her seat.

Jolene set her cigarette in the ashtray and picked up the loaded shotgun off the kitchen table. She leaned back in her seat and aimed the gun at the doorway. Larry's work boots sounded heavy as he walked up the few treads of the porch and made his way to the front door. Jolene heard him pause and then turn the handle. Jolene's heart was racing at a mind numbing pace and she began to breathe hard in anticipation of the next few moments of her life. Larry opened the screen door with enough forced that it hit the outside wall and came back to slam shut as he stepped inside. Once inside, he didn't say a word but Jolene knew he had a short fuse and a terrible temper. Jolene was nauseated. Larry's boots carried him across the living room and down the hall towards Jolene. Jolene waited anxiously for his form to fill the doorway into the kitchen.

Larry made it to the kitchen doorway; he crossed his arms and leaned up against the doorjamb.

"What's this?" Larry asked between his grinning lips and nodded in Jolene's direction, focusing a steely gaze on the shotgun. Jolene didn't reply.

"What do you think you are going to do with that gun, Jolene?" Jolene remained silent. She sat steady and strong, considering her heart was about to beat right out of her chest and do flip flops all over the kitchen.

She shook her head quizzically and shrugged her shoulders as if her aiming a gun at him was perfectly normal. At that point in time, it did feel perfectly normal to Jolene and in a few short moments Larry was going to wish he had never laid an eye on Jolene.

"Go ahead," Larry scoffed at Jolene with a sinister sneer. "You don't have the guts!" he growled; his amusement turning to anger.

Jolene contemplated putting the gun down and pleading for Larry's forgiveness over her evil thoughts, but that lasted a split second. Unfortunately, it was enough time for Larry to approach the table and lean closer to her face.

"You little whore!" he screamed at her, while pounding his fist on the kitchen table. His spittle sprayed her nose, cheeks and chin. Jolene flinched in her seat at his anger. He reached to take the gun from her but Jodie lifted her legs and placed her feet onto the table legs and pushed the table hard and knocked Larry into the wall behind him. He just missed the doorway, where he would have fallen instead.

Larry shoved himself off the wall and used his hands to push the table back at Jolene, who had rested her feet back on the floor. Jolene scooted her chair back quickly.

"Back Off!" Jolene screamed at Larry.

Larry nearly doubled over in laughter at her defiance and with his anger roiling, he lunged for Jolene. Jolene didn't pause to think. She aimed, shut her eyelids and pulled the trigger. A deadly shot rang out and the force rocked Jolene right out of her chair and onto the floor. Blood and flesh spattered everywhere. Jolene opened her eyelids and watched Larry. His face went from a shocked expression to total disbelief as his body fell hard against the wall behind him and he slid to the floor. Jolene gasped at the large gaping chest wound she inflicted on Larry and she watched in horror as the light extinguished rapidly from his eyes. His body went limp and his head leaned forward sharply.

Jolene's horror was quickly replaced by a flood of relief. Jolene stopped looking at Larry's dead body and glanced around the room. Her eyes scanned every inch of the kitchen, making mental notes of what degree of cleaning and repair needed done. After her assessment was complete, she decided to glance herself over, as well. Her face, arms, hands, the tops of her thighs and rifle were soaked in Larry's blood. What Jolene desperately needed was a long, hot shower but she knew she didn't have time for that now.

Jolene rose and wiped Larry's blood, with the back of her hand, from her face. She only succeeded in smearing the red liquid into her skin. She set the rifle on the kitchen table and began tearing down the tarps, while wrapping Larry's corpse up in them. After snuggly tucking the corpse in its cocoon, Jolene walked for the back door and went to the shed. Once in the shed, she retrieved some old nylon rope and dragged it into the kitchen behind her. Jolene tied up her package using every square inch of the fifty foot rope she had rummaged out of the shed. She made her last few ties tightly around the neck and left about ten feet free to string up to her four-wheeler.

Jolene grasped the free ten feet of rope and dragged Larry's body, by his neck, through the kitchen and to the back door. Jolene opened the door and dragged Larry down the steps and outside; his body thumping against each step and finally onto the grass.

"For someone as small as me, you don't seem so tough anymore." Jolene talked to herself out loud. No one for miles would know what happened here tonight. Jolene lived in a secluded part of the swamp. Her nearest neighbor was at least two miles down the dirt road going into town.

Jolene dropped the rope and went back into the shed to drive out her four-wheeler. Jolene used the keys in the ignition and fired up her vehicle. She revved the engine a few times and put it in drive. Jolene slowly drove out the shed door and onto the grass. She drove over to Larry's corpse and stopped just short of running over it and placed it in park. Jolene swung her leg over and hopped off the seat and onto the grass. She walked over to Larry and took the extra rope and tied the free end tightly to her hitch. Jolene climbed back on and put it in drive a second time.

Jolene drove her four-wheeler slowly through the backyard, down a small hill and onto a muddy trail leading into the heart of the swamp. Gnats flew furiously over head and Jolene swatted them often as she made her way deeper into the rotting foliage. Much to her delight, her tires and Larry's corpse effortlessly glided along the well worn trail. After reaching her destination, she cut the engine off and swung her leg over and hopped off her vehicle again. She walked around and untied Larry's corpse from the hitch. Jolene then drug Larry over to an alligator infested part and used her feet to shove him in the water. Small waves rippled the surface and Jolene noticed she wasn't the only one there.

Two alligator heads popped out of the water a few feet from the edge. Jolene watched as they eyed the neatly wrapped package that contained their evening meal. Jolene cautiously backed away from the water's edge as she walked backwards towards her four-wheeler. Jolene swung her leg over the four-wheeler and sat down in her seat. She quickly reached around to a satchel she had mounted to her vehicle and swiftly lifted the flap open. Once opened, the flap revealed Jolene's spare pack of cigarettes and a lighter. She reached down and retrieved them. Jolene opened the pack of cigarettes and watched the gator's as they swam ever so close to Larry.

Once the gator's reached their quarry, Jolene used her lighter to light the cigarette. She inhaled deeply and exhaled just as deep. She watched as the predators gnawed at the nylon cord with their monstrous teeth and clawed the tarp with their razor sharp nails. Jolene inhaled sharply and exhaled slowly, while reveling in her freedom, as the swamp devils devoured their meal.

Satisfied only when the last morsel was swallowed, Jolene flicked the remainder of her cigarette in the alligator's direction.

"That's what a little girl can do."

Kimberly Bennett

Me, George & the Flesh-Eaters

George and I had been on the run for over a year now. We were exhausted, half starved and seriously dehydrated. We were currently on the outskirts of Las Vegas and we both were not happy about it. Death lurked in every darkened door way, so we tended to stick to areas saturated with the light. Life had become very dismal, depressing and utterly hopeless for the two of us. The only thing that kept me going was George and I am sure that, without me, George would have given up a long time ago himself.

George was a red and white painted horse. He had a white star on his forehead and one white sock and he was given to me by my "Grand pap" for my sixteenth birthday. George and I became instant best friends. We were destined for each other and we always knew what the other was going to do before they did it. We had an unusual psychic connection and that link kept us alive, for the time being. I had been a typical twenty-two year old, long-haired brunette with a sassy attitude and zest for life. Now, I had cut my hair awhile ago to keep myself easier to maintain and my sassy attitude and zest for life turned into strong survival instincts that kept me running on minimal sleep and nourishment.

I lead George into the late great city of Las Vegas. We cautious eyed every building, every street, every window and every doorway. We left no crevice out. Our survival depended on our instincts and observation. The Flesh-Eaters were here. I could smell them and the way George flared his nostrils, I knew he could smell them to. Their odor was an unmistakable mixture of death and decay. They came to poach on the weak and ignorant. George and I were neither, but our time for extinction was fast approaching. I felt like something terrible was going to take place today when George nuzzled me awake early this morning. That feeling remained with me well into the afternoon and continued to nag me and gnaw at my very being up to the present moment. George must have sensed my feeling because he had been skittish and nervously pranced most of the morning and afternoon.

The city was quiet. It was way too quiet for my comfort. I was very leery of quiet because it tended to mean a storm of evil was brewing somewhere close by and it usually resulted in George and me making a mad dash to save ourselves. My eyes darted from doors, to rooftops, to windows and alleys. I was searching for the Flesh-Eaters. I wasn't prepared for George and me to become the next main course for their insatiable appetite. They were definitely predators but far worse than any predatory animals I knew about. The undead had their particular evil tendencies that I wished I had never witnessed. George and I approached a shopping plaza and scanned every square inch of the front. Our ears had become attuned to the minutest of sounds. Nothing. We found nothing to see and nothing to hear but a soft breeze whipping through the street and the stench of death.

I spied a local hair salon as the third storefront down from the end we were currently standing at. I tugged on Georges reins and guided him to the entrance of the salon. We both peered into the filthy, large double doors made of glass. I pushed on the doors and cringed as they squealed in protest but opened nonetheless. We cautiously proceeded inside. George's shoes clip-clopped on the dusty tile floor. His steps reverberated off of the walls and continued into an echo further down the back hallway. We paused and listened. Nothing. We continued deeper inside the dank and dirty establishment.

I led George over to the sink basins and pulled out a hose from the sink base and turned the water on gently. I waited until the water ran clear and plugged the sink. I could hear George's breathing become quicker in anticipation. My breathing increased and my mouth ached for the cool water to to quench the thirst I had carried with me since yesterday. George felt the same. I shut the water off, after the sink filled half way. I made a cup with my hands and began to take greedy handfuls of the revitalizing liquid and drank. I allowed the water to overfill in my mouth and dribble down my chin. George nuzzled me and I moved to the side of the basin to allow him to dip his head down and drink, as well. When I had my fill, I paused again to scan the room we were in and listened for unwelcomed movement. Satisfied with the silence and lack of interruptions, I allowed George to continue his drink while I moved over to the next sink to wash myself up a bit. I turned the water on, gently, in the second sink and plugged the basin. I watched intently as the water climbed halfway up the basin and I shut the water off. I opened the cabinet above the sink and retrieved a white towel from its bowels. I ripped the towel into fours. I placed my newly made wash clothes on the side of the sink and began to strip down. George looked up at me and shook his head while he snorted. He looked back down into the sink and continued slurping up the remainder of the water while I dowsed a wash cloth with shampoo and began to vigorously scrub myself from top to bottom. I couldn't tell you the last time I had washed. I had to have had at least an inch of dirt and grime all over my body. The filth and sweat had permeated every crack and crevice of my slender form and took all four clothes to adequately clean. I felt refreshed when I was done but very naked in more ways than one. The sun was setting and it wouldn't be long before the Flesh-Eaters would be out and about. I kicked myself for the indulgence, even though it was long overdue.

I heard a guttural growl outside the double doors. George lifted his head from the, now empty, basin and quieted his breathing to listen more intently. I raced naked to the doors and locked the deadbolt. I knew it would only be a matter of time before several Flesh-Eaters would arrive. We had a small window of opportunity to make a break for it and here I stood naked. I rushed back to the sink, slipping and sliding along the tiles to where my clothes had been tossed on the floor. I was hoping for the chance to wash them but that chance was gone. I hurriedly put my dirty clothes back on and grabbed Georges reins.

More growls and now moaning was audible. George began to nervously prance again. I stroked his mane and shushed him.

"It's ok, boy," I continued to stroke his mane. George pranced some more. I firmly held his reins and we walked to the edge of the plate glass windows and peered outside.

A Degree of Wickedness

I could see the Flesh-Eaters coming. The sun had begun to sink below the horizon and that's when the evil came out to play. I hoped that they couldn't smell us because then they would work themselves into a frenzy and we would be in more dire straits then we were at the present. It was too late in the day to take off out the front or the back, so I led George into a back room where we were able to peer between doorway cracks at the enemy approaching in the front.

George gave a soft whinny. "Shush, boy," I tried to calm George. I began to stroke his mane again, to comfort him. He quieted. More moaning and growling came to our ears. They were closer now. They were frighteningly closer. I became sick to my stomach. The hunger for food was overwhelmed by the hunger for freedom and safety. I couldn't wait any longer. I didn't know what awaited us outside the back door but I wasn't going to stick around any longer. Our safety was threatened and my fight or flight instincts were kicking in and telling me to take flight. My instincts were usually not wrong, so I went with my gut. I led George out of the back room and down the empty hall to the back door. I turned the doorknob slightly. The latch released and I pushed the door open a crack; I then stealthily hopped onto George's back and kicked my heels into his sides.

"Yaw! George, let's go!" I yelled into George's ear while kicking him into action. George took off like a bolt of lightning.

Kimberly Bennett

The back door burst open and off we raced down the darkened alley. Numerous Flesh-Eaters were out and about and that made George run all the faster. We literally ran over five on our way down the alley. They clawed and hissed at us as we continued on. I gripped George's reins tighter. I felt the night air sweep over my body and through my hair. Our escape to freedom was exhilarating but short lived. Just before we made it to the edge of the city, the Flesh-Eaters rarely left the city to venture into the desert, a net came down upon us from the last large sign on the way out of town. It was a heavy net. It stopped our flight to freedom in its tracks. The Flesh-Eaters had grown smarter. I peeked between the netting and saw two undead sitting atop the sign cheering over their accomplishment. The others came quickly and we were surrounded. There was no way out for George and me. George lay on his side with his chest heaving at his miraculous run and our impending demise. His eyes were wide open in sheer terror.

"I'm sorry, George," I whispered in his ear. I stroked his mane. I couldn't move. Pain shot through my left leg and hip like a dagger. When the net fell on us, George dropped onto his left side which resulted in trapping my leg beneath his weight. We were doomed to die a terrible death. Our flesh would be stripped from our bones while we were kicking and screaming. The Flesh-Eaters were merciless.

A Degree of Wickedness

As the evil undead crowded around our helpless forms, I struggled against the netting to reach into my satchel behind me. I opened the satchel with one hand and retrieved the pistol my "Grand pap" had given me, when the Flesh-Eaters first came. He didn't survive and now George and I faced the same fate. I cocked the gun and pointed the barrel at George's head.

"You may feast on our flesh tonight, but you won't have the pleasure of our screams and torture!" I yelled at the undead. George whinnied. The Flesh-Eaters reached down to remove the netting and I fired a single shot. The bullet pierced George's skull and his body went limp. The Flesh-Eaters began to tear at the netting furiously. A tear of sorrow slipped down my cheek. My heart broke at the sight of George's lifeless body. He had been my best friend and the only friend I had for a long time. An ache in my chest that formed at his passing almost crippled me. I ran a loving hand through his mane. But just as the undead removed the netting, I raised the pistol again and fired another single shot. This time it went through my skull.

Mr. Not So Nice

Josh Milton was a hardworking, happy man in his thirties. You could tell he was near without seeing him physically. He always had pep in his step and whistled a melodious tune that was downright infectious. Most anyone that knew him would say he was Mr. Nice; the few that would disagree never got to tell about his dark side, whether it be in life or death. Josh was an intelligent but twisted individual.

Josh liked seeing the fresh new hires faces that came through the doors of the local plastic factory that he had been employed at for the past ten years. The young women with their shyness and awkward demeanors and the young men that made him laugh with their undeniable immaturity and their unending pick-up lines. He managed to focus his attention towards a cute but standoffish blonde who seemed to be in her late twenties.

Shari gave the impression that she was a little intimidated by the work force of Johnson Plastics but mostly unsure of herself, which would account for her gruffness when spoken to by others. Josh found her attitude exhilarating and the scent of her recently washed hair to be intoxicating. He steered clear of her for now but had pegged her for a conquest at a later time. Right now, he was turning his attention towards observing and creating a plan to approach her without coming off overbearing.

******

Shari had noticed several times that Josh Milton was eyeing her and sizing her up and she didn't like it one bit. There was something off about Josh that she couldn't quite put a finger on. His charming personality was overwhelming to her like the stench of rotting garbage and her intuition was solidified when he finally had the nerve to approach her and ask her out on a date. Shari looked into his eyes and saw a darkness there that bordered on sinister. He made her feel uneasy and bile had a habit of coming up in her throat, which she managed to fight back down, when she thought about him or had to speak to him. So, Shari decided not to spend any time on thinking about Josh or talking to him and ignored his advances, which lasted a work week, and then he finally seemed to give up.

The next week seemed to start without a hitch but Shari began to feel rundown before lunch break. Shari didn't know how she was going to finish the night by the time her last break came around. Her throat was scratchy; she was chilled and had developed an annoying cough accompanied by the feeling of dizziness. Shari managed to stumble through the last quarter of her evening and was relieved when it came to an end and the midnight shift came on. She quickly packed up her things and headed for the front of the building. Once there, Shari hurried to the time clock, clocked out and walked out the door. What she didn't know was that someone lurked outside in the darkness waiting for her.

*****

Josh reflected on his observance of Shari and mentally recorded Shari's demeanor and pasty complexion at the beginning of the shift to the end of the shift. He watched as her condition worsened as the evening wore on. He knew if he was going to make a serious play he should do it tonight, while she appeared in a weakened state. So, Josh paid close attention to Shari most of the night. He watched how she wiped at her fevered brow frequently and how she tugged at the collar of her t-shirt every time she coughed.

A Degree of Wickedness

Now that work was done for the evening, Josh waited for Shari. He watched as his fellow co-workers left for the evening. He hid in the shadows and waited patiently. Josh watched intently as Shari drug her sick and weakened body to the time clock, punch out and make her way out of the building and into the darkened parking lot. He cautiously eyed her sluggish movements as she made her way to her car that was parked at the far end of the lot.

As Shari rummaged around her backpack for her keys, Josh sprung into action quickly. He sprinted quietly through the parking lot to her side. As he forcefully grabbed Shari from behind, she let out a startled gasp. Josh gripped her tightly and clamped a hand over her mouth. He then drug her kicking and flailing to the back of the building and around the corner. He shoved her roughly up against the outer brick wall with enough force to knock her unconscious. Her limp body slid down the wall and fell with a thud to the ground. Josh bent over and lifted Shari's body and carried her to an unattached storage unit at the back of the building that the company rarely used. He bent over and layed Shari's body on the ground and fished for the storage unit keys, that he lifted from the foreman's office the previous evening, and smiled when he found his prize. He removed the keys from his pocket and inserted them into the lock. He turned the keys in the lock while simultaneously turning the door knob. The door creaked open and he bent to pick up Shari's body. He lifted Shari up in his muscular arms and carried her over the threshold. Once inside, Josh flicked on the light and kicked the door shut.

The lights flickered for a few moments and then came to life. Shari began to stir in Josh's arms. Josh walked to the center of, the nearly bare, storage unit and placed Shari on the ground at his feet. He scanned the dirty unit and his eyes caught on to a shelving rack to his right. The rack had boxes of unopened shrink wrap and he quickly decided that that would be perfect for rendering Shari unable to escape. Josh raced to the rack and reached for a box of shrink wrap. He pulled the box towards him and violently ripped the packaging tape off. He opened the box and pulled out a roll of shrink wrap. He loosened the edges of wrap from the roll and pulled some free. Shari moaned and stirred on the floor and Josh moved quicker. He took the roll of wrap over to Shari and furiously unrolled it while wrapping her up like she was in a cocoon. Before Shari was fully conscious, Josh had managed to wrap her body up entirely, leaving her neck and head exposed.

Josh watched as Shari opened her eyelids. She choked back a cough as she began to sob.

"What are you doing to me Josh?" Shari asked with a quivering voice; her eyes wide with terror at her predicament.

Josh looked down at her with an evil sneer. "Why couldn't you just have said yes, Shari?"

"I'm sorry Josh," Shari replied with tears streaming from her eyes. "We..we can go out now," she stammered nervously.

"Sorry, sweetheart. It's too late for that now."

Josh enjoyed their banter but was becoming bored of it and wanted to complete the task at hand; to get his mind numbing rush. Josh turned a deaf ear to Shari's pleadings for mercy. He extracted his work knife from his back pocket and bent over Shari. She screamed a shrill scream as he raised his knife and slashed her throat wide open. As she began to choke, blood gurgled in her throat and cut off her scream. Shari tried desperately to squirm out of her bindings but to no avail. Blood spurted from her gaping wound while coating the plastic as it then ran in rivulets to the floor.

Josh reveled in his conquest and unzipped his pants, took out his erect shaft and began to masturbate over Shari's almost dead body. He stroked himself harder than usual as her life-force drained from her body and a pool of blood turned into a pool and a stream. When he reached climax, Shari's body gave a final shudder and her eyes glazed over as she released her soul from its shell. Josh pointed his stream of squirting seed at her body and made a trail from top to bottom until he was completely devoid of semen. Satisfied with his accomplishment, he smiled an evil smile while tucking his member back inside his pants. Josh then blew Shari's corpse a kiss, turned and walked to the storage unit door. When Josh reached the door, he crossed over the threshold to the outside and into the darkness while shutting the door behind him.

Darkness engulfed the inside of the storage unit and Shari's lifeless body was left to rot, alone.

Conversation with a Corpse

"Greg," the Medical Examiner called. "Get your butt over here and wash this body before I get back from lunch."

It had been a long tiring morning, for intern Greg Somers, at the county morgue. Greg sighed heavily and trudged over to the table where the body of a young woman lay dead. The M. E., Dr. Stevens, was an overweight and burly man with a short fuse. It didn't take much to set him off, so Greg gathered items quickly to get his appointed task done.

Greg walked over to a cleaning closet as the M. E. walked out the door. The closet was at the far side of the room and as he reached for the cabinet door handle, the fluorescent bulbs began to flicker.

Greg looked up and watched the flickering bulbs pulse slowly then the pulses became more rapid until the bulbs began to blow apart one by one. Greg instinctively raised his arms over his head to protect his face from the shards of glass raining down upon the room.

"Shit!" Greg exclaimed. "How the hell am I going to explain this?"

Once the bulbs were done bursting, Greg put his arms down and began to brush himself off. He immediately walked over to the door where the wall phone hung and dialed maintenance.

"Hey, can I get someone down here to replace some bulbs?" Greg spoke into the phone. "All of them blew at one time. I've got a real mess to clean up!" Greg reached up with his free hand and rubbed his forehead. "How am I supposed to know? Maybe we had a power surge." Finished with his conversation, Greg replaced the phone receiver in its cradle.

Greg scratched his head as he scanned the entire room one more time. He had better get a move on if he was going to have the room and the dead woman cleaned up by the time the M.E. came back from lunch; if not, there would be hell to pay.

Greg walked over to the where the dead woman lay. Each of his steps made an eerie crunching noise as he went. He approached the table with the woman on it and pulled back the sheet. He looked at her pale face and shook his head in disgust. Her blonde hair lay in damp strands on the table like a halo about her head. Greg pulled the sheet completely off of the woman, exposing her entire body. He instantly developed an erection. He noticed she had strangulation bruising around her neck and a few bite marks on her upper thighs. Other than the markings, she was a very curvaceous and beautiful young woman.

"Lady, you are too fine looking and young to be dead." He said to her.

Greg walked down the side of the table to her feet and picked up her toe tag to read her name. If he was going to become intimate with her by washing her body, he had to know her name.

"Nicole R. Durn," Greg read out loud to himself. "Nikki, who would want to hurt you?" The question remained unanswered in the silence of the morgue.

Greg walked back up towards her head and stopped to admire her facial features. He then turned and went to the closet for a second time to gather the items that he needed. Once he claimed the items and grabbed a rolling tray, he returned to Nicole's body. Greg placed everything on the tray except a small bucket that he took to a nearby sink to fill with water and disinfectant. After filling the bucket he went back to Nicole's body, picked up a wash rag and dunked it into the solution.

"What the….?" Greg's question hung in the air. As he wrung out the rag and turned to begin, he noticed Nicole's eyelids were open wide. Startled, he jumped back a few steps and knocked over a nearby aluminum cart. The rattle of the cart falling to the floor echoed eerily through the morgue and caused a chill to run up Greg's spine. Greg cautiously approached Nicole's body, while staying focused on her eyes.

"Greg," a whispered voice said. Greg's eyelids enlarged and his breathing grew ragged as his anxiety level skyrocketed. "Greg," the whisper came again.

Greg gulped hard and gathered the courage to answer back. "Who is it?" he asked.

"Nicole."

Greg gasped in horror to the reply and with a shaky hand he rubbed his forehead in bewilderment.

"Don't be scared," Nicole said.

"What the hell am I supposed to be?"

"I have to tell you something important."

A cool breeze blew through the morgue and brought about goose-bumps to Greg's flesh. He stood for a second before saying anything. "How can you talk to me if you're dead and your lips aren't moving?"

"I am feeding off of your sexual energy," Nicole replied. The comment brought a bright flush to Greg's face. "I'm speaking to you telepathically." Greg raised his eyebrows. "I'm stuck in between your world and the realm in which I need to travel to."

"Why are you stuck?"

"I have to tell someone what happened to me or I can never pass completely from a mortal existence to the next life."

A Degree of Wickedness

"Ok, go ahead then." Still very scared and unsure of the situation, Greg decided that if he was going to get any work done then he better let Nicole say what she had to say. He began to wash her body as she began recounting her painful story.

*****

My alarm clock buzzed its unwelcomed wake up call. The incessant sound encouraged me to blink my eyelids open. I stretched an arm out from under my covers and reached over to the clock to shut the alarm off. I recoiled my arm back under my covers. Enveloped in warmth, I was hesitant to get up and start my day. My whole body was racked with dull aches after the previous night's lovemaking. My lover was a rough one from time to time. I didn't mind much but the first few times were hard pills to swallow. I slowly come to realization that roughness was part of our intimacy and I had better accept.

I lay for awhile tucked in my cocoon. I glanced at the clock; it said it was well past ten a.m. and I needed to get cleaned up. I groaned in protest but managed to fling off my covers and sit. I then stood up and walked to the bathroom to take a shower.

As I washed, I contemplated our relationship. Crazy as it sounds; he is invisible. He has visited me every night since I moved in two months ago. I had no choice in our first encounter, when he forced himself on me. I had been scared out of my wits and thought I was going mad but the throbbing between my legs told me that what had happened was real. Every encounter after that was consensual. He is a very skilled lover. I have to admit, him being invisible lends to a mysteriousness that I find exhilarating and quite sexy.

My infatuation with my lover was a deciding factor for my decision to end my life, to be with him eternally. At this point, there was no way I could exist without him by my side. I would be lost without him. Once I finished my shower, I dried off and went to my bedroom to dress.

After dressing, I decided to gather what I needed to make our relationship permanent. I went to the living room and jerked out the phone cord from the wall jack and phone. I also picked up a chair from my eat-in kitchen and made my way back to my bedroom. I placed the two items down on the floor at the foot of my bed and I slowly sat down on the edge of the mattress.

I contemplated the ramifications that my action would bring, but my determination was solidified when I thought about being without my lover and how my heart would break and my body would wither away to nothing without his touch. I bent over and picked up the phone cord. I then stood on my bed and wrapped one end of the cord tightly around my ceiling fan base. I hopped off my bed and strategically placed the chair directly under the fan. I glanced at the clock. It was nearly noon. It was time for me to prepare my last meal.

A Degree of Wickedness

I trudged to the living room and into the kitchen. I rummaged through my refrigerator and cupboards. Once I found what I wanted to eat, I placed everything on the counter and began to prepare my meal. I enjoyed the aroma of a good cut of steak frying in the skillet with onions and garlic. A potato was cooking in the oven; smothered in butter and wrapped in tinfoil. As I waited for the familiar sound to announce it was done, a bowl of buttered broccoli spun around the microwave.

While I waited for my food to be ready, I bustled about the apartment tidying up. Once my cleaning project was complete, I sat down in the living room on the couch and cried. I cried at how I thought my parents and friends would get along without me and how my co-workers would feel once they heard the news of my demise.

The microwave dinged and I jumped with a start. I wiped the tears from my eyes and cheeks with the back of my hands as I rose from the couch and finished preparing my meal. I sat down and enjoyed every morsel before putting my dishes in the sink. Once I was finished in the kitchen, I headed back down the hall to my bedroom. I walked through the doorway and over to the chair. I stripped my clothing off and carefully stepped up onto the chair. I grasped the phone cord that dangled from the ceiling fan and tied a noose knot. I then pulled the cord over my head. I closed my eyelids and waited with anticipation for my lover. It didn't take long for him to arrive. I knew he was in my bedroom, when a cool breeze blew in from the hallway and wrapped its icy fingers around my body. I felt a gentle caress on my inner right thigh and then I felt his invisible hands lift my leg and drape it over his shoulder. I felt his breath on my skin and let my head fall back while he began to nibble his way to my fold. At first, he glided his tongue around the outside, then he sucked fervently at my button and last, he began to probe my inner flesh with his tongue. This went on for several moments as I moaned with pleasure. Time stood still for me until the volcanic rush of passion reared its head and blazed a path from my nether regions up to my skull. It exploded into a rush of fluid and heavy breathing. My knees became weak and while I struggled to stand, the noose became tighter; causing my desire to build again.

I felt my lover remove my leg from his shoulder and then he whispered in my ear. "What are you doing?" he asked.

"I want to be with you for eternity and the only way I can accomplish that is by dying," I replied.

I heard a deep laugh erupt from him and reverberate around the room. I felt him at my side and then the chair was kicked away, causing my body to drop and the noose to tighten. I instinctively reached up and clawed at the cord, to no avail. I gasped and choked for air and as I hung strangling to death, my lover laughed again.

"Stupid woman," I heard him say. "You are no good to me dead."

A Degree of Wickedness

My eyes grew wide with fright as I continued my struggle.

"I feed off your sexual energy and when you die I cannot manifest myself anymore."

I was down to my last moment.

"It doesn't matter. I will find another."

*****

By the time Nicole finished her story, Greg had managed to wash her entire body; with the help of the emergency flood lights. He stood for a few moments trying to absorb Nicole's story. The heartbreak and horror of sacrificing yourself for love and then be betrayed in return was terrible. Nicole had paid the ultimate price and had it thrown back in her face. Greg glanced down at Nicole's body and noticed her eyelids were closed again. The breeze that blew through the room was gone and panic set in as Greg realized that the M. E. would be back any minute and he still had to clean up glass.

Kimberly Bennett

The Fatal Fortune

Rebecca's designer high heels clicked across the well worn wooden porch as she walked up to the front door. The flamboyant sign that hung off to the side read: Fortunes Read by Madam Ligeia, palmistry, tarot cards and crystal gazing. Rebecca paused a moment to gain her composure. She felt odd standing on Madam Ligeia's porch, yet here she was. She never really believed in fortune tellers but a co-worker encouraged her to visit Madam Ligeia and this peaked Rebecca's curiosity. Rebecca was recently engaged and her upcoming marriage left her feeling anxious. She felt that it couldn't hurt to see the fortune teller and maybe something good would come of it. Rebecca reached out with her index finger and pushed the door bell button.

A Degree of Wickedness

*****

I was straightening up my home before my first client showed up, when the doorbell gave me a start. I walked briskly to the door, grasped and turned the old glass knob on the front door and opened it. The door creaked slightly as I pulled it open completely for the young woman to enter.

"Come in Rebecca," I said encouragingly with a sweet smile on my face. "Follow me." I led the woman through my front room and into my dining room, which I had converted to my reading room. The soft scent of jasmine that clung to my client was lost in the aroma of incense that I had lit prior to her arrival. The fragrance of vanilla and lavender dominated my home, helping to create a relaxed atmosphere for me to get to work. The more relaxed and trusting my clients are, the more money I tend to make.

As we entered the reading room, I motioned for the young woman to have a seat in an antique Queen Anne occasional chair that my Mother had handed down to me when she passed away last winter. The arms and legs of the chair were a rich hue of mahogany and the upholstery was a brilliant shade of royal purple. My chair, which sat directly across from hers, was identical. The young woman gracefully sat down in the chair and slowly leaned forward, while resting her hands on the table.

I walked to the far side of the room and closed the heavy drapes for privacy and to set the mood of the room. After closing the drapes completely, I took time to smooth them out. I turned from the window and observed my client from the corner of my eye. Her eyes darted about the room nervously as she began to fidget in her seat. Her hair was a honey blonde shade and shimmered in the soft light of the single lamp that set on the side table against the wall to my right. I took a few steps to my chair, across from the woman, and pulled it out from the table.

"Would you like a cup of chamomile tea?" I asked before sitting down.

"Yes, please." The young woman smiled at the offer and seemed to relax a bit.

"Please give me a moment." I turned and left the room and made my way to the kitchen to make the tea.

Once in the kitchen, I didn't bother to turn on the light switch. There was just enough light coming in the window over the kitchen sink for me to see adequately. I opened the cupboard door to the left of the sink and grabbed a tea cup and saucer. I smiled as I recalled when my Mother first gave the tea set to me as a housewarming gift when I purchased this small home. I sighed deeply at the loss of her and snapped out of my reverie. I placed the saucer on the counter and brought the cup over to the sink. I turned the faucet on and tested the coolness of the water with my index finger. Satisfied, I put my finger to my mouth and licked the water off. I then filled the tea cup with the cool water, shut the faucet off, placed the cup in the microwave and turned it on.

A Degree of Wickedness

While I waited for the familiar ding of the microwave, I rummaged through my cupboards for some sweetener packets and tea bags. After finding what I was looking for, I placed the items on the counter and shut the cupboard doors. As I prepared the tea, I lost myself in thoughts of my relationship with my lover, Christopher. I had some premonitions lately about our relationship and it made me feel uneasy. Even though our lovemaking was always very passionate, something was off and I couldn't quite pin point it. Once I was done making the tea, I made my way back into my reading room.

"Thank you for the tea," Rebecca said as I placed the tea cup on the table in front of her.

"Your more than welcome," I graciously smiled at her. I walked over to the other side of the table, pulled out my chair and sat down. The soft glow of the lamp light illuminated the small room with its warmth and created an atmosphere of relaxation.

" Let's get started."
Rebecca nodded in agreement, picked up her tea cup and gingerly sipped from it. She sighed heavily as she swallowed the brew and placed the tea cup back on the table. She extended her left hand, palm up to me.

I gently grasped Rebecca's hand and began examining her palm. "Hmmmm, your heart line starts in between your index and middle finger."

As I told Rebecca about her heart line, I traced a finger along it to show her where the line began and where it ended. "This indicates that you give your heart away to easily." Rebecca nodded her head in agreement at my explanation. "Your head line, which is below the heart line, is broken in several spots and very wavy."

Rebecca looked at me puzzled; I went on. "This waviness indicates that you think about several different things at one time, thus making it difficult for you to concentrate on only one." Rebecca raised her eyebrows. "The broken spots indicate that you are not consistent in your thinking, as well." Rebecca sighed heavily at the determinations. I traced a finger from one edge of her palm and downward. "Your life line is deep, which is a good sign you are healthy, but it is broken in a few places." I looked up from her palm and looked into her bright green eyes. "Your life line concerns me." Rebecca now furrowed her brow at my words, with good reason. I went on to explain that the broken spots would indicate some serious events that have taken place or would take place in her lifetime. Concern creased Rebecca's forehead and tears welled up in her eyes as she withdrew her hand from mine. She looked down at her hands and then glanced across the table at mine. Her angst turned into surprise as she reached for my left hand and fingered my engagement ring. Immediately, I noticed what she noticed; we shared the identical ring. I wanted to smack myself for missing the similarity when I examined her palms.

"Our rings match," Rebecca stated.

"Yes, they do," I replied. My curiosity was piqued by the rings and I felt compelled to ask

A Degree of Wickedness

Rebecca a burning question. "Do you have a picture of your fiancé?"

Rebecca looked at me with surprise at my question but reached into her purse without a word and shuffled about for a moment and finally pulled out a photo of her and her fiancé. She handed the photo over with a sweet smile on her face. I grasped the photo from her and turned it so I could see it better. To my horror, what I found in the photo changed the course of Rebecca's young life. Entwined in each other's embrace, was a very beautiful Rebecca and a very dashing man who was my fiancé, Christopher. Their eyes were locked in a gaze of lust and their arms encircled each other's waists, pulling them closely together. A rage engulfed my being at the betrayal and its venom coursed through my body destroying my sanity in its wake. I tried to compose myself as best as I could and handed the photo back to Rebecca with a shaking hand.

"Very nice," I said with a forced smile.

Betrayal was a bitter pill that I had to swallow for the moment. I took a few deep breaths and watched Rebecca return her photo to the depths of her designer purse. I briefly pondered what my course of action would be. My thoughts ran rampant through my mind as I tried to tame the beast that burned to escape from my control. I must find a way to rectify the situation. I couldn't live without Christopher and his love, even though his infidelity had smacked me hard in the face with Rebecca sitting across from me.

"Rebecca, I need to tell you that I get the feeling that your fiancé in the photo has another woman in his life." Surprisingly, she did not looked shocked which added to the anger growing inside of me.

"Christopher had been engaged before me," Rebecca stated. "He told me that she died a horrible death in an accident that he couldn't bring himself to explain any further."

I felt sorry for her for a split second over Christopher's betrayal of her but that feeling quickly dissipated and my previous emotions gripped me again like a vice. I decided that Christopher was going to have to pay for his infidelity and dishonesty. I also decided that Rebecca was going to play a huge part in the price that he was going to have to pay.

"I have a bad feeling about this other woman," I leaned across the table and looked into Rebecca's eyes. "I would like to give you a special necklace that will protect you from evil. Rebecca raised her eyebrows at my words and I reached over to the lamp stand and opened the drawer. I reached in and retrieved a beautiful cat's eye on a leather string. I showed Rebecca the necklace and allowed her to finger the cat's eye. The eye was a brilliant shade of lime green with flecks of gold. It was one of my favorites but I felt that Rebecca should have it. I rose from my chair, walked around the table to Rebecca and stood behind her as I brought the necklace down and around her neck.

A Degree of Wickedness

"Please wear this to protect yourself and your relationships from harm." Rebecca nodded her head at my words. I fumbled tying the leather string around her neck, trying to delay the inevitable but gave up before Rebecca got suspicious. I grasped the ends of the string and pulled it tight against her neck. Rebecca gasped in surprise and began clawing at my hands. I pulled the string tighter and pressed the front of my body up close behind her. Rebecca continued to struggle but her efforts were futile. Her nails dug deep into my hands as she fought my grip for several moments. With one last squeeze and blood dripping from my wounds, I took the breath from Rebecca and allowed her body to slump forward resting her forehead on the table. I let go of the string and proceeded to removed Rebecca's engagement ring from her finger. I then jerked a lock of hair from her head. I brushed a second lock of hair away from her face and planted a kiss on her temple.

"I'll be back later to take care of you."

*****

I collapsed on Christopher's chest and buried my face into the crook of his neck. Soaked in our sweat and exhausted by the passion we had just shared, I slowly sat up straddling Christopher's hips and leaned over to my nightstand. I grasped the knob on the drawer and pulled it open. I picked out a lock of shimmering blonde hair and a gold ring. I sat upright again and placed the items on Christopher's chest.

"I'm not the fiancé that died a horrible death," I said nonchalantly.

Christopher's eyelids flew open as he brought a hand up and picked the two items off his chest without looking at them. I smiled down at him and slowly swung my leg over and climbed off of Christopher's body. He glanced down at the items in his hand and I watched as tears slid from his eyes and down his temples, only to disappear into his hairline. I casually strolled into the bathroom to take a much needed shower as I left Christopher to ponder his actions.

A Little More Off the Top

Beth heard the all too familiar jingle of the front door bell. She sighed heavily at the intrusion, tossed a few more towels into the washer and turned it on.

"Helllooooooo," the next customer called out.

"I'm coming!" Beth shouted back.

Beth hunched over her shoulders and made her way from the dispensary out to the salon floor. She paused briefly at the restroom door, deciding whether to knock or not but went with the latter. Her co-worker Amy had scurried off to the restroom when her boyfriend showed up for lunch and by the sound of her moans and the slapping of wet, sticky bodies; Beth thought they were a little preoccupied to be disturbed. Beth shook her head in disgust and said a little prayer that they wouldn't break the sink this time because Amy was already on the verge of being fired for several past problems with her behavior. Beth continued down the hallway and emerged onto the salon floor.

The salon had a clean and modern look to it. The open floor plan made it easy to navigate around the styling stations for customers and employees alike. Beth liked the salon but she just wasn't crazy about the owner or her co-workers. They were a hodgepodge of personalities that didn't seem to fit any particular mold and many times it wasn't uncommon for tempers to flare and tantrums to be thrown. I guess you could say they were an eclectic group.

"It's about damn time!" the annoyed customer exclaimed. "I haven't got all day!"

Mr. Grey was a regular customer and a regular pain in the ass. He was the type you wish something terrible would happen to. The type you would get to read about in the paper and shake your head and say, "That is awful," and not really mean it.

Beth approached the desk and asked Mr. Grey to sign in.

"You can follow me, Mr. Grey," Beth said.

The man walked around the counter and nearly knocked over Beth trying to get to her station first.

"Clumsy fool," he muttered at Beth, as she stumbled.

Beth regained her balance and kept back a few steps in case he got any more funny ideas. Mr. Grey reached the chair first and waited for Beth to turn the chair around so he could plop his fat pompous ass down. Beth did as was expected and then draped Mr. Grey with a cape.

"What can I do for you today?" Beth asked.

"The same damn thing you always do, but take a little more off the top this time."

"Will you excuse me so I can get a clean comb from the back room?" Mr. Grey was annoyed at the question but waved his hand at Beth, like he was dismissing a servant. Beth locked the chair to keep it from turning and trudged back down the hallway to the dispensary.

The clean comb adventure was an excuse to get away from Mr. Grey for a moment and calm her nerves before starting her haircut. Beth knew she was in for a rough ride and wanted a swig of vodka to get her through. As she walked past the bathroom, she heard squeals of Amy's laughter and her boyfriend saying something about her being a goddess. An impish smile overtook Beth's lips at the goddess comment. Beth thought Amy was cute but she was far from a goddess. Beth did hear a few things about Amy being good at giving head so maybe that was what the comment was about. Beth finally made it to the dispensary and shut the door. She crouched down and reached into her oversized bag to pull out her cheap bottle of vodka. After opening the bottle, Beth took the time to inhale the toxic aroma before taking a swig. Once her nostrils had their fill, she put the bottle to her lips and downed a good amount.

Kimberly Bennett

The vodka scorched a path down her throat and into her belly. She reveled in the magical calming effect that the liquor had on her and quickly took another swallow. This time, she allowed it to sit in her mouth for a moment before swallowing it completely. The second time burned more and Beth smiled at the intoxicating rush the vodka gave her. She clutched the bottle to her chest and waited for the fire to subside.

Beth put the cap back on tight and bent to bury the bottle in her bag. While she hovered over her bag making sure the bottle wasn't visible, Beth rummaged for a breath mint. Once she found her prize, she popped it in her mouth and stood up quickly; a little too quickly. Wooziness gripped Beth and she reached out to the washer to steady herself, as a giggle escaped her lips. Beth suddenly felt better and then reached into the auto-clave to extract a clean comb. She then smoothed her hair and clothes and began her trek back to the salon floor. She stopped first at a shelf next to the door and picked up a roll of duct tape that happened to be laying there. As Beth passed the restroom door, she noticed that it was open and a foul musty smell emanated from its dark depths. She quickly strode past Amy's empty whorehouse with her hand covering her nose. She knew that Amy would be outside smoking a cigarette and waiting for the next customer to come in, leaving Beth to battle her demons alone.

A Degree of Wickedness

Beth emerged, for a second time on the salon floor and made a quick walk to her station. She tossed the comb and the tape onto the small counter as her world closed in on her. She stood a moment behind her chair and ignored Mr. Grey's babbling about his pathetic life. She was tired of hearing about the corn on his insignificant little toe, the oozing sore on his upper thigh, the weird rash on his chest and his useless wife. Beth allowed him to ramble and rant for several minutes as an invisible barrel was dropped over her. Her senses became dulled, her hearing was muffled and her breathing labored. Beth wasn't sure what was happening to her and she didn't know how to make it stop.

"Hey, dummy!" Mr. Grey snapped at her. Beth shook her head and slowly came to her senses.

"You said you wanted a little more off the top?" Beth asked.

"What the hell is wrong with you?" The snarled question made Beth feel worse then what she had. It reminded her of her father, his abusive nature, all the school kids who ever taunted her and then something snapped inside of Beth. A switch turned on that she never knew she had and anger boiled in her veins like the vodka scorching a path from her lips to her belly.

Beth turned the chair around so Mr. Grey could face her. She delivered a well placed blow to the bridge of his nose and watched the blood begin to pour. Mr. Grey instinctively brought his hands to his face and sat in stunned silence. Beth then placed her hands on either arm rest and dug her fingernails into the vinyl upholstery. She bent down so she was nose to bloody nose with Mr. Grey.

"You are what's wrong with me!" Beth gritted her teeth in anger. "You are going to sit there and shut up, while I cut your hair." Mr. Grey stared at Beth with disbelief written on his face. "Then you are going to take your fat, snooty ass out of here and never come back."

Before Mr. Grey could protest, Beth twirled the chair back around and picked up the roll of duct tape. She ripped two long pieces off and grabbed each of Mr. Grey's wrists, one by one, and secured them to the arm rests of the chair. She then picked up the comb and her scissors and proceeded to cut Mr. Grey's hair.

Beth finished the haircut expeditiously and placed her tools on her counter. She picked up a nearby mirror and held it so Mr. Grey could see the finished product. Mr. Grey inspected every inch of his haircut and after several moments had passed, he brought about a smirk to his lips.

"I need a little more off the top."

Beth was filled with rage and saw her flushed complexion staring back at her in her reflection of the giant mirror attached to her station. She didn't say a word but simply twirled the chair around so Mr. Grey couldn't see what was coming next. Beth opened a drawer on her station and pulled out her standard issued straight razor. She then removed the guard, took her free hand and gripped Mr. Grey by his bangs. She yanked his head back hard, making sure to pop a few vertebrae.

"Ouch!" Mr. Grey yelled. "What the hell are you doing?"

Beth took a few deep breaths. "Taking a little more off the top," she calmly explained.

Beth reached around with the straight razor and slashed an incision across Mr. Grey's scalp. She made sure the cut was made above his bangs so she could continue to hold him in place.

"AHHHH!" He screamed in agony. He tried to break free but Beth had a tight grip and he couldn't move his head. Beth quickly finished scalping Mr. Grey. Blood spilled down from his head and ran in streams down his face and neck; soaking the cape with crimson. Beth peeled back the flesh with a sickly suctioning sound and examined his scalp in her hand. She then tossed the scalp into a nearby shampoo basin while Mr. Grey continued to squirm. She returned her razor to the drawer, still dripping with fresh blood. After closing the drawer, Beth then grabbed her cutting shears and rammed them deep into Mr. Grey's chest and pierced his heart with their steely blades. Blood spurted in all directions. Beth released her hold on Mr. Grey and allowed his dead body to slump forward in the chair. She stepped back to admire her work and when she was done, she went over to an empty basin to wash the blood off. Just as Beth finished washing off and drying up, Amy walked in.

"What the Hell!" Amy gasped in horror at the bloody mess before her.

Beth turned away from the sink and tossed her towel into the dirty towel bin. She looked into Amy eyes and said, "He wanted a little more off the top."

Wolf Down

Sam and I woke from a brief nap and the day started like any other day; we were frightened, hunted, hungry and homeless. It seemed forever and a day since we had a full nights rest. The old rotted bridge gave little shelter from the previous night's torrential downpour. We had been enduring soggy weather for three days now. The dilapidated floor boards creaked and groaned with every step we took. The roof was missing several boards and a majority of what was left, hung precariously above us. The sounds emanating from the surrounding woods were a symphony of chirping insects, wild birds and the chattering of other woodland creatures. The river lent its musical talents to the orchestra of nature that flowed beneath our temporary home.

"Jenny," Sam whispered in my ear. "I'm going for a dip. Do you care to join me?"

I stretched and then yawned while Sam rose from his place beside me. I blinked me eyelids open only to be surprised with the vision of Sam standing before me in his birthday suit and extending a hand in my direction. His lean muscles and black wavy hair made me suck in a breath but it was his deep cerulean blue eyes that held me captivated and made my heart go pitter-patter.

I smiled an impish smile and grasped his out stretched hand in response. Sam pulled me to my feet and then released my hand from his. I turned away from Sam and removed my damp jacket to shake the excess moisture from it. I then draped it on the bridge railing and began shucking the rest of my worn out clothing. The smell of dampness and sweat hung like a heavy blanket in the air. I had hoped the rain would hold off for few days, so we could dry out a bit. I tossed my clothes to the side and allowed the gentle breeze to envelope me, then brush past my body.

"Ahhhh, that feels good," I sighed.

"Come on slow poke!" Sam called to me as he dashed past me and blazed a naked trail down the groaning bridge and then jumped through a gap in the railing to the waiting water below. I laughed out loud at Sam's total disregard for modesty and quickly followed suit; water play ensued. Our splashing and giggling echoed off the surrounding woods. After a few moments, our play took a different turn when Sam grabbed me and pulled me in close. I placed a hand on his bare chest and the action left me weak in the knees. The sexual tension between us was undeniable and I held off for as long as I could. We had been on the run for over eight months now and my desire for Sam had grown exponentially in that timeframe. I trusted him completely with my physical well-being, my heart and even my soul. I couldn't hold back anymore.

At first, our embrace seemed awkward but after a few moments of gazing into each other's eyes I could not deny the love I held for Sam. He slowly brought his lips to mine and gently sucked my lower lip. A flush rose in my cheeks and a raging flow of fire burned its way to my fold.

I parted my lips and allowed Sam to probe its warm depths with his tongue. I felt him rise to the occasion, hardening in an instant. Sam's hands began to caress my back and make their way down to my buttocks. I reached up and wrapped my arms around Sam's neck and thrust my tongue into his mouth. Our tongues danced the dance of lovers and the moment almost seemed magical.

Sam's caresses turned into urgent kneading of my flesh and I knew he couldn't wait any longer. I raised my legs in the water and wrapped them around his hips. His strong arms held me up as he guided himself into me. I had never known a man until now and once the sharp shooting pain from his initial thrust subsided, we fell into a comfortable rhythm. The rippling water around us lapped at our flesh like a thousand hungry lovers and sent shivers of delight up my spine.

We parted lips as Sam emitted a soft groan. His momentum increased just as the pressure of passion rose and began to rage within me like a rabid beast of its own design. Sam's breathing became ragged as my nails dug into his back. And then it started. It began as a distant tingling sensation and quickly morphed into one fantastic explosion that shook me from head to toe. I squeezed my eyelids shut riding out the moment for all it was worth. I could feel Sam shudder and release his seed into my womb like a geyser. Once I regained my senses, I opened my eyelids and reveled at the sight of Sam staring into my eyes like the satisfied lover that I felt like. I was mesmerized by his deep blue irises and my gaze lowered to his sensuous lips, stained red from our intimate encounter.

"I love….," I placed an index finger to his lips and silenced his announcement. I winked at him and retracted my finger.

"I know."

I released my leg lock on Sam as he extracted himself from me and we parted. We both swam in silence to the edge of the water and crawled out onto the grass. We both lay face up and stared into the sky. I felt so free and happy laying next to Sam. We didn't need to touch our look at each other to know what had grown between us and that what had just happened in the water was only the beginning of something beautiful.

The faint sound of hunting dogs in the distance brought us back to reality. We both sat bolt upright and snapped our heads to look at each other. Fear and anger was etched on Sam's face and we both knew what that sound meant. Sam and I hopped up and raced to the bridge to dress. A shot rang out nearby and just as we made it to the bridge, Sam dropped down to the ground with a thud behind me. I stopped dead in my tracks and turned to see Sam with a bullet hole in his right shoulder at my feet. His hand gripped his shoulder to staunch the flow of blood. Panic rose within me but I pushed it back down; now was not the time to lose it. I reached down and helped Sam to his feet.

We crossed the threshold of the bridge and grabbed our clothing, just as the hunters were closing in. Before we could dress, I heard the hammer cock in a gun to the left of the bridge. My eyes shot over to the side and a gasp escaped my lips as I saw a hunter standing there in the tall grass taking aim at us.

"Look what we have here," the hunter commented as several other hunters emerged from the woods and approached the bridge with their rifles leveled at us; "The wolf and his bitch!" The other hunters grunted in agreement.

Sam charged the first hunter and was immediately brought down by another silver bullet, this one entering his left shoulder. Sam writhed in pain at my feet. Both wounds smoked and hissed incessantly while his cursed blood oozed from the gaping holes. I dropped to my knees to comfort Sam.

"I say we have some fun with the bitch!" another hunter exclaimed, taking in my nakedness with lustful eyes. Several of the other hunters nodded in agreement.

"Don't you touch her!" Sam growled. He briefly looked into my eyes and flashed his inner wolf. I nodded no to him but he transformed anyways.

As a few hunters approached closer, Sam instantly turned from human to wolf. His black coat gleamed in the sunlight and his wolf eyes blazed with anger. He snapped his sharp canines at them and they all jumped back a few steps. In that instant everything became silent. There was no more nature's symphony and no more comments from the hunters. Sam leaped in front of me with his massive body, shielding me from the perverse gazes of the hunters. He meant business. Even with his wounds, Sam was still a formidable foe to come against as the wolf. Sam let out a ferocious howl that split the air like a freight train barreling down its tracks. The hunters began to advance on us; determined to end our existence right then and there. Sam jumped into battle and managed to toss a few hunters to the side, like rag dolls. Pain was etched on Sam's face but he continued his onslaught of violence.

I stood back, unable to help him in the least. I was not advanced enough with my curse to completely transform in an instant. I watched as several shots were fired from rifles but no bullets found their mark. Sam strategically leaped from one victim to the next; either he snapped a neck, snapped them in half, or ripped the hunter's throats out with his claws. The bridge and surrounding area became soaked in crimson.

Even though I stood a little distance back on the bridge, I became spattered with the hunter's blood, as well. Another shot rang out through the air and I gasped in horror as I watched the bullet strike Sam in the forehead.

As quickly as the battle begun, it had ended. Nausea overtook me and I vomited over the side of the dilapidated railing. Sam's head had been completely blown off his body. My world ended and my heart shattered into a million pieces. Sam's headless body stood still for a moment and then fell to the ground with a sickening thud. I raced to his side, dropped to my knees and began to sob uncontrollably.

I was oblivious to the hunters advancing on me and Sam. I was inconsolable. It wasn't until I heard some boards creak on the bridge behind me, that I turned and bared my sharp canines. Fury flashed in my eyes as I lunged at the closest hunter. The last thing I heard was the all too familiar sound of one last gunshot.

Kimberly Bennett

Potion of Betrayal

I fell to the floor with a thud and smacked my head on the hardwood flooring; pain shot through my skull that caused me to wince in agony. It must have been some type of poison that I had ingested. My stomach churned with nausea and my veins felt like they were on fire; the fire spread from my stomach into my limbs and up into my head. My arms and legs became too heavy and I was unable to move. Everything began to look foggy and the sounds around me became muffled. I was drifting away and could do nothing to stop myself. I felt utterly helpless.

My pulse began beating wildly out of control and the pounding in my head could be heard in my ears, as well. My whole body was engulfed in a burning sensation. Not a sensation that was unbearable but one that needed quenched as soon as possible.

My life didn't flash before my eyes like I thought it would. My anger grew as I lay dying, moving from a conscious to an unconscious state and back again. I was betrayed and I knew exactly who was responsible. It was a pity that I could not do anything to bring about justice. I knew that it was too late for me.

Through my drug induced haze, I saw my murderers face before me. My eyes were opened just enough to take the image in. She had an evil grin spread from ear to ear and she laughed a mocking laugh. I hated her. I truly hated her. She had been my childhood friend and our relationship was born out of co-dependency. She was bossy and I was timid. Her aggressiveness gave me power in some strange sort of way. Sometimes I felt like a leech clinging to her very core for survival.

I had met her when I was a scant eight years old. She was the new girl in town and I did my best to make her feel welcome. I was the only one to play with her at school or ask her over afterwards for dinner at my house. The other kids did not like her and I was never really sure as to why. I guess she just rubbed them wrong.

As we grew into young adulthood, her features became more beautiful. She had charm and there was an authority in how she spoke and carried herself. I knew why other girls despised her then. They were jealous of her appearance and the fact that she was adept at handling boys. She would snatch boyfriends away, use them and discard them. Boys were literally afraid of her after our first year in high school but that didn't deter her from seeking out other conquests. She had quickly moved on to young college men when we entered our junior year. She was 17 but acted and looked like she was in her mid-twenties, so men were an easy prey.

By the time we graduated the twelfth grade, she had gone through a string of young men and was on the prowl for more. She was eager to go away to college and resume her hunt without parental eyes following her every move. She had plans, big plans. She was an aspiring attorney and nothing suited her more than that.

My eyes are watering. Why are my eyes watering? I can smell smoke. It is faint but I can smell something burning. I couldn't feel heat because my body still had a burning sensation from the poison, but I knew the place where I was must be on fire.

I can hear movement around me like shuffling furniture. I am too groggy to open my eyelids, but my smell and sound senses are intact. My limbs are still useless, so I can't move at all. It feels like I have heavy weights attached in different spots on my body that prevent me from any type of movement. I was beginning to wonder when it was all going to end and then I think about her, again. I think about her and the fire in my veins subside and I pick up my thoughts where I had left off.

A Degree of Wickedness

*****

She took my lover from me out of a desperate attempt to squash any happiness that I might forge out of my life. He had been the very heart and soul of my being. I loved him dearly and would do anything to protect our relationship. She was jealous at what she couldn't have and set out to destroy my lover and me. She drove a wedge between us by spinning a vicious web of lies and half-truths and then moved in for her take over at his weakest moment. Her time to act came when I had been away on a business trip. I had only been gone a few days, but that was all she needed. She arrived at his home with alcohol in hand and seduction on her mind; the second night I was away. I give him credit for trying to resist her at first because in my heart I know he did, for he loved me just as much as I loved him.

We hadn't been talking for two weeks over her disgusting version of a business dinner we had endured the night before. She produced pictures that were pretty incriminating but he never gave me a chance to explain. He flew into a rage and that was that. I had never seen her follow me and I was not aware she was even there at the restaurant. But she had made sure that whatever happened would be blown out of context.

*****

Smoke is filling my lungs with its kiss of death. The smoke is becoming unbearable and now I can feel a searing heat. I am sure my body and all the evidence that points to her will be destroyed and she can then go on her merry way with my lover in tow.

Tears begin streaming down my face. They are not tears from irritating smoke but from a pain so unbearable and so uncontrollable. My heart is breaking and I can never seek out my revenge. In a few moments, I will be nothing but bones and charcoaled flesh. It feels as if a sword has been driven through my chest, twisted, pulled out and drove in again just for good measure. My death will be the end of my physical agony and at this point, it couldn't come soon enough. But my death will start a new chapter in my betrayer's life. I could waste my time thinking about how I could destroy her but what is the use when I will be dead?

*****

I had come home earlier than expected from my trip and in the mood to reconcile, only to find them in his bed. They were entwined with one another under the covers and sleeping peacefully. My heart sunk at the sight. I woke them with a bloodcurdling scream that could have awakened the dead. They both jumped out of the bed and stammered out an explanation that just would not satisfy me.

I slapped her in the face and knocked her to the floor. I vowed she would pay for her wickedness.

A Degree of Wickedness

She lay there rubbing her cheek and glaring at me. She swore to me right then and there that she would pay me back for that night. I scoffed at her and kicked her hard in the side. She lay curled in a heap and whimpered in pain. I then turned to my lover and spat in his face as he climbed out of our bed and dropped to his knees, naked, and wept with shame. He cried out apologies and words of love flowed from his lips. I wasn't buying it and I was too angry to hear him.

*****

The heat and pain is becoming unbearable. I can smell the fabric of my clothes burning and it is definitely an unmistakable smell. The fire has quickly claimed my clothes and is now working on my body. My flesh is slowly blistering and melting off my body and I can't find enough energy to scream.

I am not sure how long I have left, but I know it's not long. I maybe have a few moments or so.

No, not even that..........

The Possession

I felt his presence before I had seen him, as I fumbled for my house keys at my backdoor. I had a long day at work and played just as hard this evening at the club with my friends. It was two a.m. and all I wanted to do was take a shower and crawl into bed. While I searched for the house keys, I had a strange feeling someone was behind me. I turned my head to look and no one was there but I knew someone was waiting beyond the porch light and enveloped in the darkness. I hated that creepy feeling, so I moved quicker to find my keys. It seemed like eons before I finally felt them at the very bottom of my purse. I pulled out the key ring and just as I was about to insert the backdoor key in, I dropped it to the ground. I bent to retrieve the keys from the concrete driveway, when I saw a shadow move out of the corner of my eye. I stood upright and turned again to see no one was behind me but I knew better. I turned back around to try the lock again and he came up behind me. A strong arm encircled my waist and pulled me close. I could feel a cool breath on my shoulder as a man's hand brushed my hair away from my neck. The breath moved from my shoulder to my neck.

"I have been watching you for a long while," a deep, sensual voice whispered into my ear. "I don't want to hurt you."

As crazy as it sounds, I believed him. I was frozen in time. I couldn't muster even the slightest protest at the embrace. I was scared but I couldn't scream, I couldn't run and I couldn't fight. As my body rested on his chest, his hand caressed my neck tenderly while a shiver crawled up my spine but it did nothing to motivate me into action. I felt the pressure of teeth bear down upon my flesh and then they pierced my skin like tiny needles and punctured my jugular. The pain was instant and it radiated down my arm and up my neck into my skull, simultaneously. I managed to writhe in his grasp for a moment and then I collapsed into his embrace. I knew my life force was being drained away and that I was powerless to stop it as it ran in rivulets down my back.

My attacker moaned in ecstasy as he drank from my body. The whole experience was just as erotic as it was frightening and lust began to pulse through my body. My knees grew week and I began to slide to the ground but before I finished my decent I was shoved up against the side of my house and propped up by the pressure of a male body against my back.

I could feel his erection through the back of my dress; his hardened shaft rested between my cheeks while desire burst through my veins like a bullet fired from a gun. He separated himself from me just enough to slide a hand into the top of my dress and caress my right breast. The attacker nestled his face in my neck and breathed in my scent. He moaned in pleasure and slid his free hand down further on my body. He slipped his hand quickly underneath my dress and pushed his fingers past my panties. He stroked my fold inside and out until I shuddered with delight at his touch. He circled a finger around the entrance and then delved inside. He stroked my inner sanctum until I could feel hot, sticky moisture weep from between my legs and a tingle in my belly erupted into a full-fledged orgasm that rocked my body into a senseless state. I instantly grew weaker in the knees as my whole world exploded within me in a fantastic display of inner fireworks. In one swift motion, he then picked me up and cradled me like a baby in his strong arms. The movement was comforting and terrifying at the same time.

My eyes were wide open and as the man carried my body towards the garage and through the backyard; I could see the familiar outline of my house disappearing rapidly. His movements were fluid and almost like he was gliding on air. The cool, night air began to dry the blood that had run down my back but the heat and moisture remained fresh between my thighs.

I heard a car door open and the man placed me inside a vehicle. The cool fabric of the upholstery on my back began to give me the shivers all over again. The man slid in the vehicle and raised my head and rested it in his lap. I heard him give the driver instructions through a rolled down window between the front seat and the back and then the window rolled shut leaving me alone, once again, with the man. I'll admit that my catatonic state was disconcerting. I was placed on my back on the longest seat and I watched as the street lights whizzed by. My breathing seemed steady but I couldn't feel my heart beating. I would panic but I couldn't muster the energy to get the job done. My limbs were useless and my rationalization seemed to be dwindling. A hand began caressing my hair, I looked up and could see the man moving his blood encrusted lips and I could hear words but I couldn't understand what he was saying. Sound had changed from being crystal clear to muffled and monotone. I'm not sure what was to become of me but I didn't think it was going to be good.

We drove down street after street and past the city limits and into the country. We turned onto a gravel road surface and I could hear the crunch of rocks underneath the tires. Each jarring of the vehicle brought about a more intense pain to my head and neck. Life had taken a dangerous curve for me and I was uncertain as to my future. The city lights had long since dropped from my sight and darkness now engulfed not only the vehicle I was traveling in but my very soul, as well.

No Mercy

I sat atop the roofline peak awaiting sunset; my perch was directly above Michelle's window. I had watched her grow from an even-tempered infant to a rambunctious pre-teen. Her bubbly spirit and compassionate demeanor made her worthy of my protection. Her fair hair, paired with her porcelain skin tone, truly gave her a look of innocence.

The sun began to slide into the horizon, creating a beautiful display of watercolor streaks of pink, orange, purple and red that gave way to a darkening sky. A few more moments and nighttime will be fully underway and my prowling will start anew.

I could hear Michelle dancing about her bedroom preparing for bed. Her stereo serenaded me with its melodious pop number that I was sure she had not listened to in quite awhile. The sweet scent of vanilla wafted up to my perch from Michelle's open window. I inhaled the soft aroma vigorously, as well as her shampoo and soap. I could envision her hair still damp from her evening shower, her pajama's on and her hairbrush being used as a microphone as she danced all over her large bedroom, trying to squeeze out the last ounce of her energy before hitting her head to her pillow.

Darkness enveloped the neighborhood with its ominous appearance. Michelle had since turned her bedroom light on and the amber glow of her lamp spilled out of her window and onto her balcony before losing itself in the night.

"Goodnight, Michelle!" her mother called to her from somewhere downstairs.

"Goodnight, Mom!" Michelle breathlessly replied. Michelle switched her lamp off and I could hear her crawl into bed and cover herself up. I glanced through the inky black across the street and scanned the area for Michelle's neighbor. The lonely man who lived across from her house gave me a very bad vibe. I didn't trust him. I watched, from my perch, every day as he eyed Michelle and her other female friends. There was something about that man that spoke evil to me. The man across the street watched Michelle's every move that she made outside of her home. I have observed him watching her leave her home, walk with friends to the bus stop, walk home and even entertain her friends in her front yard. He had a vile spirit and I had seen lust in his eyes on more than one occasion. I feared for Michelle's safety, especially during the day. I was unable to protect her during the day but when the sun went down and darkness covered her home, it was game on!

The sun had now disappeared completely into the horizon and the night sky blanketed its darkness evenly over the neighborhood and it was my time to prowl. I yawned and stretched each of my limbs. As I stretched, crumbling of rock could be heard. I shed my daytime shroud and brought forth my living self. I could feel my circulation coming to life in my veins but I was careful to keep the noise level down, as Michelle was not in a full slumber yet. I could hear her breathing go from rapid deep breaths down to slow and shallow breaths as she began her REM cycle.

I scanned the yard for potential intruders but all I could spy was a few nocturnal insects buzzing about and a field mouse on the hunt for a late night snack. Satisfied, I tilted my body slightly forward and gently glided from my perch down to Michelle's balcony railing. I stretched out my claws and gripped the cold, hard metal railing, as I landed. I cautiously peered into Michelle's bedroom window and quickly glanced around the room. It seemed safe at the present, which allowed me to relax for a moment. I knew that the night was just beginning and I had a bad feeling about things all day. Something had set me on edge but I wasn't quite sure what it was. I turned my face up towards the night sky and took in the familiar scent of a storm brewing. Lightning flashed in the distance announcing its up and coming arrival.

The moonlight streaming into Michelle's bedroom left an otherworldly glow in its wake. My grotesque form was duplicated on Michelle's wall and gave me a start, once I had noticed it. I carefully gazed into the darkness of Michelle's room to check on her sleeping form. Her bed was on the opposite side of the room as the window. I inhaled sharply and took in the sweet, innocent atmosphere of her bedroom. I watched as she stirred in her sleep and slowly rolled from her left side over to her right. She gently nuzzled her pillow and pulled her legs up close to her abdomen and she then became still again.

The moonlight that spilled into her bedroom, from the outside, poured silvery shafts of light across her hair giving it an iridescent appearance; while her exposed skin seemed as if someone had sprinkled glitter all over it. Her delicate facial features seemed more angelic in her restful state, which made me want to protect her all the more.

Out of the corner of my eye, I noticed a strange movement in the yard and did an about face on the railing. I quickly scanned the yard for potential danger as my hunting skills were awakened and fully functional. I know I had seen something and adrenaline blazed a fiery path through my veins. There it was again. I leveled my gaze directly at the object and spotted the man across the street creeping his way towards Michelle's house along the side yard that was lined with trees.

I was now attuned to the minutest of sound and fully alert. The man had vanished from my sight once he made it to the corner of the house but I still was aware of his presence because I could hear his movements and smell evil emanating from his being. I kept my post and continued to listen for him in the dark and dreary night.

I could tell by the sound of rustling leaves that he was encroaching upon the back door and then I heard breaking glass during a loud thunderclap. Lightening immediately streaked the sky and the rain came down hard. I sat silent as the man's footsteps echoed down the hallway. The man was stealthy and he moved cautiously through Michelle's home, but I was well aware of his intentions and knew I couldn't let them come to fruition.

I noticed a creaking noise coming from the floorboards from the other side of Michelle's door. I looked into the darkness that filled her room and watched her still body sleeping away the day's events. I drew my gaze to her door as the knob began to turn slowly and it was pushed open just as slow. His ominous figure stood in the doorway as lightening flashed and a thunderclap reverberated off of the walls in Michelle's room. I watched as he crept into her room and made the few steps to her bedside. He stopped and bent over Michelle's bed and hovered over her helpless body. Just as he was about to reach out and touch her, I sprang into action. I glided swiftly through the window and landed directly behind the man. He must have caught my movement and turned around quickly. Before he could gasp in shock, I grasped him by the neck with one large claw. I watched as disbelief, surprise and then dread flashed across his features while he tried to process my existence in his sick mind. I single handedly lifted him from the floor. He struggled by kicking his legs and pulling at my claw around his neck, but his efforts were futile. I smirked at his wasted movements. I carried him across the plush carpet over to the window, while his eyes grew wide with fright and at the realization that this was not a dream or his imagination running rampant but something very real. I passed through the window with the man in tow and leapt up onto the balcony railing. In one quick and sure motion I flung myself into the night sky, taking him with me. I spread my massive wings and flapped them a few times, so I could hover, than I descended slowly to the water soaked earth. We landed with a sloppy splash in some mud and I brought my wings close to my body. The man squirmed in my grasp some more; I decided to slam his puny body into the ground with my one claw and knock the wind from his lungs with the force I used. I glanced up at Michelle's window and detected no movement and then returned my attention to the man, again. More lightening streaked the sky and the rolling thunder covered his pleas for mercy. I had no mercy for this one. I was going to make sure he could never hurt another person again, including my Michelle.

*****

I woke with a start. My heart pounded furiously in my chest. I knew something wasn't right. I opened my eyelids and sat bolt upright in my bed. I gasped in horror as I saw a grotesque animalistic figure dragging a second, more human, figure out my bedroom window. I quickly placed my hand over my mouth to squelch any sound from escaping my lips. My eyebrows rose in amazement over the scene that was unfolding before me. I shut my eyelids and rubbed them vigorously, with the back of my hands, several times. When I reopened my eyelids the two dark beings were gone. Hastily, I flung my covers off and raced to my window. I watched as the animal creature used his wings to descend from my balcony and land on the soft ground below; his skin glistening in the moonlight. In one razor sharp claw he held a human form by its neck and I watched as he slammed the body into the ground, hard. My eye's quickly adjusted to the night and I could make out the figures a little better. The animal creature appeared to be the gargoyle that sat on my rooftop and the human was definitely my neighbor across the street. I gasped again in horror at the situation, but I was left helpless and unable to stop anything. My fright held me frozen on my balcony.

I watched helplessly as my neighbor clawed and kicked at the creature, while he laid on his back. The gargoyle raised his free claw and with a slashing motion he sliced my neighbor's torso open from throat to belly. Blood spurted from the gaping wound and was diluted by the rain that continued to fall. I watched as intestines spilled from my neighbor's abdomen and I held back vomit as the gargoyle released him from his grasp and began dining on his innards. The gargoyle gobbled up every last morsel before turning in my direction. I quickly ducked below my window and prayed he didn't see me.

I crouched on my floor in terror; not over the death of my neighbor but in how he had died. The man across the street scared me. I'm not sure why but I didn't like how he looked at me or my girl friends. There was something odd about him that never sat well with me.

I gathered the courage to stand, close and lock my window tight. I then made a bee-line for my mother's room and crawled into her bed. "I had a horrible nightmare," I whispered in her ear. She rolled over and wrapped her arms securely around me and hugged me close. I felt terrible that I wasn't sad for the man across the street and I felt odd when my horror over the gargoyles actions slowly gave way to an understanding of some sorts. In my mother's comforting embrace, I prayed that I would wake and what I saw was just a horrible dream.

The Death of Gyn

Amber was a homely, young girl whose lot in life was to troll around the local truck stop, on the outskirts of town, for reluctant johns. She frequently staked out the parking lots from behind truck trailers and waited for opportunities to present themselves. A drunken driver sitting over night and waiting for the morning was her best bet. Sometimes she would have to perform sexual favors for cash and sometimes she just had to hang with the driver and wait for him to pass out from alcohol and then Amber would pick his pocket and be on her way.

Amber was what society deemed as worthless trash but little did they know, that by the end of the night, she will become a slayer of evil and quite possibly save us all.

A Degree of Wickedness

*****

Work was slow tonight. Rainfall had a habit of drawing in the driver's but tonight was odd. There were barely any tractor trailers parked for the evening. Disgusted with the evening's prospects, I walked alone through the parking lot towards the diner that stayed open all night. The neon blinking red "Open" sign hurt my eyes with its pulsing light as I opened the glass entrance door. The dimmed lights of the diner were a welcoming change, once I was completely inside.

Burnt coffee filled the air with its pungent aroma and the smell of cooking grease added to the typical truck stop diner atmosphere. I stuck my hand inside my jacket pocket and fished around for some change. I walked over to the diner counter and sat on a stool. Gail, the waitress who was usually on at night, let me have a piece of pie and a cup of cocoa for fifty cents. I smiled a bit when my fingers found their prize. I quickly drew out the two quarters from my pocket and tossed them on the diner counter and waited for Gail to come by. As I waited, I shucked my jacket off and hung it on the back of my chair to dry.

Gail finished filling a straggling trucker's coffee mug, took his money and said goodbye. He left hurriedly without returning pleasantries. Gail just shrugged it off and made her way over to me. Her frizzy red hair and pale complexion, plus the annoying habit Gail had of snapping and popping her gum, did nothing for her. I could tell she had already had a long evening, even though it wasn't over yet. It was only one hour past midnight and Gail's shift wouldn't be over until six.

"Would you like the usual, sweetie?" Gail asked me with a weak but welcoming smile.

"Yes, thank you," I replied. Gail busied herself preparing my hot cocoa and slice of pie. My mouth watered at the thought of food, any type of food. I hadn't eaten all day because I was waiting for pay from a john that I had serviced at nine this evening. He was my only customer since yesterday. Pickings were slim and I was desperate, so I did what no hooker should ever do; I took an I.O.U.

Gail delivered my goodies and picked up the change I tossed on the counter. "Gail," she stopped walking and turned to look in my direction. "Where are the truckers at?" I asked.

"Sweetie, haven't you heard about the strange disappearances we have been having lately?" Gail asked me in reply.

"No," that was the gospel truth. There maybe a few other prostitutes that trolled this lot with me but we never talked. Prostitutes do not make good friends, so I liked to keep to myself. Come to think of it, I hadn't seen the others for a couple of nights. I guess they moved on and found better pickings in the next town.

Gail sighed and trudged back over to me. She leaned in close and whispered in my ear. "The police say there is an animal loose nearby and it has spooked truckers and hookers alike but if you ask me, I think it is Cyn"

"Who is or what is Cyn?" I asked.

Gail rested her forearms on the counter and leaned in closer as she began her horror filled tale, at my insistence. "It is said that a woman named Cyndel Moore lived in this town as one of the first settlers. She met and married a man who ended up leaving her destitute and heartbroken over his philandering lifestyle. The pain of her loneliness drove her straight into despair. After a year or so, she embraced her loneliness on the outskirts of town in a tiny run down shack. After a short time, her heartbreak turned into something evil as her sanity spiraled out of control. She frequently snuck into town at night and pilfered whatever she could, just to survive. The townspeople eventually caught on and one night drug her from her shack to a nearby field and stoned her to death."

"That's terrible!" I exclaimed in disgust. Gail nodded her head in agreement and continued her story.

"A year after her murder, a strange bird-like creature emerged from the local woods and terrorized the town for a month. People described the creature as having a womanly figure covered in feathers, a large wingspan, long dagger-like talons and a very foul odor. The creature appeared at night and stole food from the townspeople and was even seen on occasion to pick up and eat dead animals along the road. Also, folks claimed the creature chased some undesirables that chose to sleep in the streets at night."

I gasped in horror at Gail's tale but encouraged her to continue. "Go on," I said.

"Some people believe that when Cyndel was murdered that she went to hell and begged Satan to help bring about justice for her untimely death. Satan granted her wish and turned her into a hideous beast called a harpy and allows her to return from time to time to terrorize the people who live nearby. Up until this year, she just stole food, chased the homeless and ate road kill."

"I wondered what changed for Cyn to make her attack people." I asked out loud.
"I have no idea sweetie but with the disappearances happening and no one acknowledging Cyn's existence, I think it is best to hunker down and wait it out. Until her existence is admitted and a plan formulated to rid the town of her nastiness, then no one is safe as long as she is here. Please be careful out there, sweetie."

I nodded my head in acknowledgement and heartily dived into the pie slice. After a few bites, I paused eating and picked up the coffee mug and took a long hot sip of cocoa. The warmth hit my mouth like a volcano and spread its soothing comfort down my throat, into my chest and on down to my stomach. I set the mug down and resumed eating my pie slice. After finishing my little piece of heaven, I turned around on the stool to glance outside the glass windows. To my relief, I noticed that the rain had ceased its deluge. Finally, I could shake off the dampness and dry out.

Gail had disappeared into the diner kitchen and I could hear her rustling about the metal cupboards. "Bye, Gail," I hollered in her direction. I heard a loud crash and some expletives issued in the form of Gail's voice. I shook my head in amusement. Gail always became clumsy this far into the evening. I waited a few brief moments for her acknowledgement and when she didn't reply, I grabbed my jacket from the back of my chair and headed out the door. No doubt, by the sound of the ruckus in the kitchen, Gail has a mess to deal with. As I opened the door, a chill swept in and brought about goose bumps on my skin like a bad rash. I shivered and put my jacket on. I reluctantly stepped out into the unbecoming night and let the entrance door close swiftly behind me.

I walked quickly towards a black semi parked along the fencing. Carl would be waiting for me, as usual. Carl was a regular john for me. He was always nice; he paid me up front without a hassle and didn't want anything weird. As I approached Carl's truck, I noticed a strange shadow cast on his driver door, brought about by the dim parking lot lights and I wasn't sure what else. I quickly walked to Carl's truck, opened the unlocked door, climbed the ladder and peered inside. Carl wasn't there.

"That's odd," I said out loud to myself. I covered my face with the sleeve of my jacket as a foul odor permeated the air with its stench. "Yuck!"

I climbed inside the cab of Carl's truck and decided to wait for him. Maybe he went to the restroom or was taking a shower. He shouldn't be long and I knew he wouldn't mind if I sat inside his truck and waited. There was no way I was staying outside with that stench floating around.

"What the….," my words trailed off as I saw something large fly over the truck and cast its shadow on the hood. The glare of the parking lot lights obscured a clear view of whatever it was and caused my anxiety level to rise. I began to think about Gail's urban legend.

I gazed out the rain spotted windshield and jumped back in my seat when a creature landed abruptly on the hood. It had a woman's figure but was covered in the feathers of a bird, instead of human skin. It crouched down and peered at me through the glass, cocking its head to one side and then quickly to the other. It was hideous and fascinating at the same time but my fascination turned to frozen with fright when the creature began to beat the glass.

I sat in disbelief for a moment as the creature pounded and clawed the windshield of the semi. Her razor sharp talons left deep scratches in the glass and her fists left spider web cracks in their wake. I shook my head to snap out of my mesmerized state. I suddenly realized it would only be a matter of minutes before the creature could get at me and I needed to do something now if I was going to survive the night.

"Where the hell is Carl!" I yelled to the birdlike creature.

A Degree of Wickedness

A steady resolve claimed my psyche and I furrowed my brows in determination as I gazed out the crackled windshield and then down at the dashboard. I gripped the well worn steering wheel with one hand and turned the key with the other. I carefully balanced the clutch and gas pedal while bringing the truck to life. I revved the trucks engine a couple of times and floored the gas pedal, making sure to switch the gears as quickly as the truck would allow me. I was heading for the truck wash at the far end of the truck lot.

I looked up from the dashboard of the truck and watched Cyn as she ceased her attack on the cab of the truck and struggled to grip the hood. Once Cyn dug her fingers into the metal hood, she raised her eyes and our stare down began. I was determined to survive at all costs and Cyn was determined to get her hands on me and end my measly life. As I increased my speed, the battered glass crackled more in protest and a putrid odor seeped into the cab; forcing me to gag back some vomit that rose in my throat. The foul odor was a combination of rotting food and human decay. As I approached the truck wash building, I forced my attention away from the foul odor and back on the task at hand. I had to destroy Cyn before she destroyed me.

Cyn began clawing her way up the hood of the truck and used one hand to reach around and beat on the window glass of the door. I shuddered at each fist pound and began weaving the truck to try to shake Cyn off. She dug her fingers into the hood and began bleeding profusely from the torn metal that now dug into her digits. She then squawked at me with a high pitched sound from her rather large beak.

I continued to weave the truck. Cyn hung on. The truck wash building came up fast and I barreled the truck into its cement block side causing my head to hit the steering wheel hard and Cyn to fly off and smack the wall. Steam billowed from the front of the truck and I sat in stunned silence, trying to regain my composure. I felt blood oozing from a gash on my forehead and a sharp pain ripple up my ribcage.

Cyn lay motionless on the truck hood. I wasn't sure if she was dead or not. I reached for the door knob and opened the door. I watched Cyn as I stood up on the step by the driver door. I poked my head between the door and the truck cab. Cyn stirred. Panicked, I got back in the cab and locked the door. She was slowly coming to and I had to finish the job. Cyn raised her head as I put the truck in reverse. I backed up with enough force that Cyn's body slid off the hood in her weakened state and slumped to the ground. I revved the truck engine and continued to back up until I could see Cyn's body on the ground. She seemed bloodied and beaten up but not quite out of the picture. She pushed herself up from the ground and stood staggering for a moment.

Cyn shook the haze from her head and glowered at me with fury in her eyes. She clenched her talons and jumped onto the shredded hood for a second round. To my advantage, Cyn couldn't get a good grip on the truck. I revved the engine and ground the gears into submission, as quickly as I could. I headed for the truck wash building again. This time, Cyn didn't have her grip and fought to stay balanced on the hood. She floundered for a moment and slipped down the hood. I watched as her talons gripped the grill in front and I floored it; ramming the wall for a second time. I heard a sickening crunch and popping sound as I crushed her body against the cement block. I didn't stop with ramming the wall; I forced the truck on through to the next wall. There the truck would go no further. Steam rose from the grill while blood and oil pooled underneath the truck.

I fumbled with the door of the truck and managed to get it open after several moments. I climbed down from the cab and walked to the front of the truck on unsteady legs. Cyn's foul odor saturated the air and hung over everything like a heavy blanket. It was almost overwhelming but I had to see her body, or what was left of it. Her talons still clung to the grill but her body was nothing but a mass of blood, gore and feathers. She was unrecognizable and nobody would believe me, but she was dead.

Bibliography

http://www.buzzle.com/articles/palm-reading-learn-how-to-read-palms.html

http://www.ehow.com/how_2052921_palm-reading.html

The Werewolf Book: the Encyclopedia of Shape-Shifting Beings by Brad Steiger

A Degree of Wickedness

About the Author

Kimberly Bennett is a recently published independent author whose main goal is to provide readers of fiction a thrilling and memorable experience when they pick up one of her books and begin to read.

Kimberly has been a lifelong resident of Northeast Ohio and currently resides in Williamsfield, Ohio. Kimberly attended and graduated from Kent State University where she earned a degree in Computer Technology.

Kimberly's second short story collection, A Degree of Wickedness, was released in October 2011. Since releasing A Degree of Wickedness, Kimberly has been promoting her book at various conventions near her home and Pittsburgh, PA.

Kimberly Bennett

Other Writing by Kimberly

Twisted Delights: A Thrilling Short Story Anthology is a collection of short stories, mostly in the present tense, including fresh ideas and old classics that have been updated with new and intriguing twists.

In a crumpled, helpless heap I sob uncontrollably and soak the bed with our shame, washing away the love that had been made just a few moments before. When I have finished with the onslaught of tears, I rise from our bed to start a fire in the hearth. I strike a match and throw it onto the leftover lumber from the night before. The wood is well weathered and dry all the way through. It lights easily, and I begin to prepare my bath for the coming evening alone. ---- Excerpt from **Until Forever**

The plane shuddered a few times, and I gripped my seat a little tighter as the nose tipped up toward the heavens. The plane evened out, and we were well on our way to sanctuary. Anywhere but back there is where I wanted to be. Even with the occasional jarring of the plane, due to turbulence, my nerves were much better off than on the ground. ---Excerpt from **No Means No**

Book Review Comments:

I can sum it up in two words; delightfully, brutal! My personal favorite being, *Aisling*.
Author/Taressa Klays

The bittersweet feeling is indeed **Edgar Allan Poe'ish**, and I felt the thrills similar to when watching **Vincent Price** staring at us with cold, indecipherable eyes.
Moderator of The Fiction Factory/Web Examiner

You can visit Kimberly and learn more about her writing at: http://kimberlybennett.yolasite.com

Kimberly Bennett contributed an original short horror story, *Hades on Ice*, to the Big Book of Bizarro.

"Salacious - Sacrilegious - Scatalogical - Scotomizing - Strange!"

The Big Book of Bizarro brings together the peculiar prose of an international cast of the most grotesquely-gonzo, genre-grinding modern writers who ever put pen to paper (or mouse to pad), including:

NIGHT OF THE LIVING DEAD horror writers John Russo & George Kosana

HUSTLER MAGAZINE erotica contributors J.T. Seate, Eva Hore & Andrée Lachapelle, and

Established Bizarro genre authors D. Harlan Wilson, William Pauley III, Laird Long, Richard Godwin and so many more!

A Degree of Wickedness

From Alien abductions to Zombie sex, The Big Book of Bizarro contains OVER FIFTY STORIES of the most outlandish transgressive fiction that you'll ever lay your capricious and curious hands upon!

WARNING: This book may be one of the most controversial and dangerous books you'll ever read.

Release Date July 29th 2011

Kimberly Bennett

What's in the Works?

Kimberly is currently working on the first novella in a series titled, *Evil, Under the Microscope.*

The series surrounds a beautiful, yet witty geneticist, Fiona Sheridan. In the first novella, *Unholy Union,* Fiona stumbles upon a plot to pollute the human race with DNA from fallen angels when her ex-husband uncovers an ancient burial ground where the cadavers of Nephilim have been discovered. Fiona races to her ex's side to take DNA samples of the discovered bodies and finally prove their existence.

When Fiona gets back home, she is summoned to a nunnery where one of the clergy, Amadora, has been raped under strange circumstances and has become pregnant with what is believed to be a Nephilim.

❖ Will Fiona be able to prove the existence of Nephilim?

❖ Can she help Amadora and her unborn child?

❖ Will she be able to stop the DNA plot in its tracks?

Expected Release Date: December 2012

A Degree of Wickedness